BROWNSTONE FACADE

By the Same Author
Edith Wharton's New York Quartet

BROWNSTONE FACADE

CATHERINE M. RAE

A
Joan
Kahn
BOOK

ST. MARTIN'S PRESS/NEW YORK

Design by Design Oasis

Library of Congress Cataloging in Publication Data

Rae, Catherine M., 1914–
    Brownstone facade.

    I. Title.
PS3568.A355B7   1987   813'.54   87-16363
ISBN 0-312-01004-4

A Joan Kahn Book

First Edition

10 9 8 7 6 5 4 3 2 1

For Gene

ACKNOWLEDGMENTS

I would like to thank Mary Rae, M. D., for her help with medical matters, David Rae for his legal advice, Kent Bloomer for his kind assistance with architectural terminology, and Penelope Colby of The Guilford Library.

BROWNSTONE FACADE

—the old obediences that were
in my blood.

—Edith Wharton

In the fall of 1968, after my aunt's estate had been settled, I found myself in possession of not only a considerable amount of money, but also her personal effects. When I came across the following manuscript in the lower drawer of a locked file cabinet and riffled through the pages, I was surprised to see my own name mentioned. I replaced the papers in the large brown enevelope in which she had left them and took them home with me. I stayed up half the night reading them, glancing up from time to time at the Bachrach portrait of Aunt Grace. Taken when she was in her early twenties, it reflects an attitude that was characteristic of her all her life: she isn't smiling in the picture, but she looks ready to smile, and there is a faintly amused expression in the dark eyes (they were the deepest blue-violet imaginable) as if she were posing merely to humor the photographer, not because she wanted a picture of herself. Her dark brown hair, with its reddish glints, which she refused ever to "bob," is arranged in a manner that provides a soft frame for the high forehead and the almost classic modeling of her features.

Even as an old woman she was remarkably attractive; those marvelous eyes were, if possible, more striking after her hair turned white, and her skin retained the creamy texture of her youth.

"I may look fine, Charles," she said with a little laugh when I complimented her on her appearance the last time I had tea with her, "and except for this wretched arthritis I guess I am. But I'm lucky it's just in my knees, where it can't be seen. I'd hate it if my hands were deformed. I do miss the long walks I used to take in the park, though."

She sounded a bit wistful then, but after a moment she brightened up and began to talk about the house she was taking for the summer at Westhampton, and how she wanted me to bring Elissa and the children down for a long visit. We never went, though; a few days after that conversation she suffered a massive stroke from which she never regained consciousness.

The events she wrote about took place during the winter of 1920–21, the year my parents, my brother, Francis, and I spent in the brownstone house. I was only eight years old at the time and understood very little of what went on. I remember being sent up to bed early on several occasions, being taken to my maternal grandmother's house—being deliberately gotten out of the way. This was probably just as well, considering how young I was and what horrors were involved. My aunt's manuscript made everything clear to me, but more than that, it presented an unusually poignant picture of the lives of the last of the New York Victorians, lives hobbled by waning but still powerful societal taboos and strictures.

It is with this last thought in mind that I have decided, now that everyone directly concerned with the events of that winter has died, to make public what she wrote.

Charles Millerton

March 1981

November 1961

When I dream, as I do from time to time, of that dreadful winter, I invariably wake up with a pounding headache, one that lasts two or three days. Dr. Bronson, who has always been ultraconservative as far as drugs are concerned, has given me some mild palliatives, but they have had little appreciable effect. The last time I went to his office I requested something stronger to relieve the pain, although I knew he would be reluctant to give it. I did not, however, expect the emphatic refusal I received.

"Damn it all, Grace," he exploded, "your problem is psychological, not physical. Strong drugs would do more harm than good in your case. Now look—"

"But you can't know how bad the headaches are," I interrupted. "My head simply—"

"Listen to me, my dear. And please believe that I know the root of your trouble. You are haunted by the past, and it must be laid to rest, gotten out of your system. Drugs won't do that, but I have an idea about something that will. I want you to sit down at that beautiful rosewood desk of yours and put on paper everything that happened that winter—not what happens in your dreams, but what actually took place. Leave nothing out; you can't hurt any feelings at this late date. Include every last detail, so that it's all written out and not left festering in your mind. You won't have to show it to anyone, not even to me, so tell it all. As I said, no harm can be done now, no reputations will be tarnished. And come and see me when you've finished it. You are still a beautiful woman, Grace; get this out of your system and enjoy the rest of your life."

With that he glanced at his watch and stood up. It was not like him to hurry me, and I'm not sure whether he was pressed for time that day or whether he wanted to forestall any objections on my part. Also, I've noticed that he's been rather brusque since his wife's death last spring. Maybe that's part of it. In any case, I had no alternative but to thank him as graciously as I could (I was far from satisfied with the visit) and take my leave.

I do not like being pushed into anything and I very nearly ignored his advice. But this afternoon I feel at a loose end: it's a cold, rainy day, not a day for shopping on Fifth Avenue, not a day to call on one of my friends—most of them have left New York for Florida anyway—and certainly not a day for a walk in the park. Time was when I would have relished a trip to the zoo on such a day (it's almost deserted when it rains, lovely and quiet), or a few hours with old favorites in the museum, but no longer; the dampness bothers my arthritis now.

So I shall try to follow his instructions. It will probably take me some time, and in order not to rush it I propose to write a section—or a chapter—a day, until I come to the end. If the dreams and headaches are exorcised, it will have been worth the effort. I cannot begin with the deaths, though. I shall have to go back a bit in time to the events that led up to them.

1

Looking back, I think the house itself, much as I enjoyed the early years of my life there, was part of the trouble. It was a tall brownstone, five stories in all, on the south side of Sixty-fifth Street, just off Lexington Avenue, and not readily distinguishable from the houses on either side of it, indeed from most of the buildings on the block. A few of the houses, including the one next door to us, were no longer privately owned, having been made over into flats, an early sign of the deterioration of the neighborhood. Since ours faced north, the front rooms were generally dark and rather cheerless during the day. They were at their best in the late afternoon or evening when the lamps and fires were lighted. The entire house was really quite dark, with windows only in the front and back. I do not think it was ever too clean, either; I don't see how two maids could have kept all five floors and the staircases swept and polished, even if they worked at it twelve hours a day, which, of course, they did not. The cook never cleaned anything but her pots, and the laundress, who came in by the day, had her own duties.

In this connection there was a story that never failed to amuse my father (although I think it rather distressed my mother) about a silver fox neckpiece that could not be found when the guests were leaving at the end of an evening party in midwinter. It was not until Easter Sunday, when children were scampering all over the house hunting for eggs, that it was discovered in the dark corner at the turn of the stairs leading down from the parlor floor to the dining room. What particularly delighted Papa was that the child, whoever he was, kept shrieking that he had found the Easter fox, a much more exciting animal than a rabbit.

But to get back to the house: I'm not sure when it was built, but I was born in it in 1895 and I don't think it was brand new then. It still stands now, in 1961, and from the outside looks very much as it did when I was young, although the front stoop has been taken down and it is no longer a one-family house. In the winter of 1920–21, the time I want to write about, we still had no electricity. My parents were so accustomed to gaslight and oil lamps that they saw no reason to have the place torn apart in order to install electric lights. They were getting on in years then, and since we all tended to humor them no one urged them to make the change.

Like most of the other brownstones on the block, our house had an areaway, an open space next to the stoop four steps below the sidewalk level, onto which the single, large dining room window opened. To the left of the window a door was set under the stoop, a necessary entrance for tradesmen, since there was no other way for them to get through to the kitchen at the back of the house. The long hall that led past the dining room, past the staircase and the built-in closets underneath it, ended at the entrance to the big kitchen with its large coal range and smaller gas stove. Behind the kitchen there was a miserable yard, used only by the laundress and innumerable stray cats.

On the second floor, a dark space known as the music room (because of the old-fashioned upright piano in one corner) separated the front and back parlors. Of these two rooms, the one in the rear was the more cheerful, since it faced the south, but unfortunately its heavy drapes were generally drawn and the sliding doors kept closed unless there was a special party. As a result, the room always had an expectant, unused look. Perhaps that is why my rosewood desk is still in perfect condition; it used to stand against a wall away from the windows, as an objet d'art, I suppose, because no one ever sat at it to write anything.

The front parlor was the everyday one. I think one might compare it to the family room of today. It was somewhat crowded with sofas, chairs, and tables, and never very tidy. Books, magazines, and newspapers were apt to be piled up on the tables, while workbaskets with their contents spilling out were either in full view on the floor or partially hidden behind the overstuffed chairs. There was generally a cat, too, even two or three cats, lying in front of the fireplace. Without them, the house would have been overrun with mice. The largest one, and by far the best mouser, was a stately, aloof female with the absurd name of Pumpy. We never could agree on the origin of her name, and as children would argue about it, but we all acknowledged Pumpy's superiority over the other cats. It hadn't taken her long, for instance, to discover that if she laid a dead mouse at Cook's feet (and waited patiently for the woman to stop screaming) she would be rewarded with a saucer of cream, something the other cats never realized.

There was a comfortable coziness about that front parlor, especially in the late afternoon. I can still see Mamma standing at the window watching for old Mrs. Fitzgerald's Packard to draw up in front of the house. The moment she saw it coming she would call out excitedly.

"Ring the bell, ring the bell!"

That was the signal for Cook to start browning her own homemade bread over the coal fire. She held each piece on a long toasting fork, and the moment it was the right shade she'd pass it to one of the maids so that it could be buttered while still hot. Toast today, made in all sorts of automatic pop-up appliances, suffers greatly in comparison with the slices that were rushed up from that old-fashioned, inconvenient kitchen. No matter how much Cook prepared and then wrapped in a damask napkin, no matter how few people were there for tea, there was never enough. And Mamma refused, always, to send down for more; the reason she gave was that we might spoil our appetites for dinner, but I really think she was afraid of upsetting Cook.

Pumpy knew better than to beg for tidbits; I remember how scornfully she looked at the younger cats when they started rubbing against one's legs and looking as if they might jump up on a lap. As likely as not, they would have to be put out of the room, and when this happened, Pumpy, my father always said, would nod in satisfaction.

I have had a succession of cats over the years, even though I live in an apartment (a lovely bright one, with southern and western exposures), but I've never had one who could hold a candle to Pumpy. She was not an affectionate creature. On the contrary, she was apt to resist any display of tenderness with a flick of her tail or a low but definite hiss. I think that's why we were all surprised when, later on, she spent long afternoons letting Rose stroke her. But I'll come to that . . .

I haven't finished with the house: my parents' bedroom was directly above the front parlor, while Rose and I shared the one in the rear. In between there was a large bathroom, which could be entered from either room or from the hall. Caroline had the back bedroom on the fourth floor, and Tom and Will occupied the one in front. Poor Alfred had to make do with a small cubicle known as the hall bedroom, also in the front of the house. The top floor was given over to the maids, with Cook in the large room in front and Katie and Maggie in the two small bedrooms in the rear. There was a bathroom on each bedroom floor, but no convenient powder room for guests downstairs.

If this sounds like a crowded household, it was, but by 1920, the year I was twenty-five, my brothers and sisters had all married. I had thought I'd be married by then—but I'll come to that later, too. Caroline, the oldest, lived a few blocks north of us with her husband, Dr. John Pelham, and her four noisy children. Papa called them "Carrie's brood," and spoiled them dreadfully. Alfred was the next oldest; he married Ann Kittredge, a beauty and a bit of a snob. She insisted on living as close to Fifth Avenue as possible ("A good address means so much, don't you think?"), and I know there were times when Alfred was hard put to make ends meet. He was a bright young man, good-natured, easygoing, and, I always thought, overly anxious to please, no matter what the cost to himself. They had two quiet boys, Charles and Francis.

After Alfred came Tom and Will. Only a year separated them, and they were as close as twins while they were growing up. No one was very much surprised when they married two sisters and set up house practically next door to each other up in the seventies. We all liked the Taylor girls; they had lived across the street from us, and I guess you might say we had grown up together. Tom and May Taylor used to say they couldn't remember a time when they didn't know each other, and Julia would tease Will by saying she remembered their introduction only too well: according to her, he threw a snowball at her one day and made her cry. In any case, they were four of the happiest people I have known, happy and lucky, I guess. Some of us have not had their good fortune.

I was next in line, and after me came Rose, the last one. It is still difficult for me to think about my younger sister dispassionately; perhaps this writing will help. She was three years my junior, born when Mamma was almost fifty and thought she was through with the nursery. From the time she was a little thing people referred to Rose as the "flower of the family" and marvelled at her delicate beauty. I don't think Rose was really conceited, but she learned early that her looks would get her almost anything she wanted.

She never did well in school, though. Carrie and I were the bright ones. We were sent to the Normal School, as Hunter College was once called, to get our teaching certificates ("so as to have something to fall back on"), but Rose was "finished" at Mlle. Pardeau's, a small establishment on Park Avenue, where she was taught to chatter in French and not much else, as far as I could see. Maybe she didn't need anything else; when she was seventeen she had half the young men in our circle at her feet, and Mamma had a terrible time keeping her social activities within bounds. Everyone assumed that Rose would marry well, including Rose herself.

"Grace," she said to me one afternoon as we started out on a walk, "let's go up Madison Avenue. I'll show you where I'll live when I'm married." (She must have been about fourteen at the time.)

"Married to whom?"

"Oh, I don't know yet. I mean, of course, I haven't met him yet. But I will, and he'll be so handsome—you can't imagine."

We walked north on Madison Avenue and when we got to Seventy-second Street she paused and pointed to the chateaulike structure that Gertrude Rhinelander Waldo had built but never occupied.

"Papa told me that house was built in 1898, the year I was born, and that Mrs. Waldo never lived in it. It's as if it's waiting for me. Think of all the lovely rooms, all the servants, all the parties! And I'll have a special bedroom suite for you, Grace, when you come to visit."

"I want the one with the bay window up there on the third floor," I said to humor her.

"Yes, that's all right," she said. "Because the one next to it has a balcony, and that'll be mine. I'll lean over it and wave to my disappointed lovers."

And she might have had all that; one of the wealthiest men on Wall Street asked Papa for her hand when she was nineteen. Unfortunately he was short and rotund. There were other proposals, five or six that I knew of and heaven only knows how many she never mentioned. Apparently no one was handsome enough—until she met Jack Egerton. It happened in East Quogue, a small village far out on Long Island, where we spent our summers. Year after year Papa would rent the same large, gray, shingled house near the water—the bay, not the ocean—because he considered the latter too dangerous for bathing. Everyone, Cook, maids, and all, would be bundled off to the "country" as soon as school closed in June. I think the laundress kept the cats for us. It never occurred to us that there was any place other than East Quogue for summer vacations, which only shows what creatures of habit we were and how unquestioningly we accepted our regulated lives.

I remember Mamma saying that the East Quogue house invited one to relax; I think she meant that most of the housekeeping chores, all the polishing and shining so necessary in the city house, could be dispensed with because of the simplicity of the furnishings. Wicker and rattan chairs and sofas with faded cretonne cushions supplanted the velvets and velours of New York, and braided or grass rugs took the place of Persian carpets. Nor were there any heavy drapes; a good many of the windows were bare, but a few, like those in the parlor and in my parents' bedroom, had crisp, white organdy curtains. At least they were crisp when we arrived in June, but after a foggy or rainy spell they began to droop, and by the time we left at Labor Day they hung limp and gray. We'd have been better off without them.

As in so many of the summer houses of that time the bedrooms were numerous and small, each one containing little more than a bed, a straight chair, a small dresser, and, of course, a washstand complete with basin and ewer. The room Rose and I had was slightly larger than the others, and naturally Mamma and Papa had the best one of all. I guess we needed all the bedrooms, for there were weekends when there were as many as twenty of us, and I never remember anyone sleeping on the sofa in the parlor or in a sleeping bag on the floor, as they do nowadays.

The parlor was large and comfortably shabby, but we never spent much time in it, only the rare evenings when it was too cold or damp to be out on the verandah; then we'd gather there to toast marshmallows in the corner fireplace when we were little, or, later on, to read and talk.

We all liked the dining room best. The morning sun poured in through windows that overlooked the bay, making the room as bright and cheerful as the one on Sixty-fifth Street, where we always needed the chandelier lighted, was dark and gloomy. We tended to linger over breakfast at the long, battered harvest table that ran almost the length of the room, even after Papa had finished his meal and settled himself with his paper in the rocking chair in front of one of the windows. Cook outdid herself with those country breakfasts: baskets of hot blueberry muffins or steaming piles of blueberry pancakes appeared frequently on the menu, as did bowls of wild strawberries smothered in thick heavy cream, fresh from the local dairy. Or if we hadn't picked any berries for her she'd send in rich, buttery cornbread with the platters of bacon and eggs.

As July advanced and the blackberries ripened, we would try to persuade her to bake a blackberry pie, but she thought "all those big seeds" were indigestible and refused. Instead, though, she'd make a blackberry syrup, to be poured over her homemade ice cream and served with slivers of sponge cake. I marvel now that we didn't all get fat; perhaps we burned up all that food somehow.

Delightful as the dining room was, the wide verandah that ran around three sides of the house was where we spent most of our time when we were at home. With its green-and-white-striped awnings, its pots of red geraniums, and its plethora of white-painted rocking chairs, it gave the house a welcoming air, and since it was so extensive, one could always find a sheltered corner, a sunny spot, or a place where a cool breeze blew in from across the bay, whatever seemed desirable at the time. Afternoon tea was nearly always served out there, and I remember how Mamma would shake her head and smile resignedly when she saw the array of small sandwiches and cakes that Maggie or Katie carried out.

"No matter what I order," she'd say, "Cook does as she pleases at teatime in the country."

Cook was sensible, though: frosty pitchers of iced tea or lemonade were served on hot afternoons, and if it was chilly, steaming pots of oolong tea would appear. And no one ever complained. Nor did anyone ever complain that there wasn't enough to do in East Quogue, in spite of the quiet, almost lazy life we led. Mornings were generally spent on the beach, and after lunch (the lightest meal of the day) one could play tennis or croquet, walk the mile to the little village for an ice cream cone, or lie in a hammock and read. Sometimes Papa would take us sailing in the afternoon, but after the boys were old enough to manage the catboat, he either napped or sat on the verandah with Mamma.

He often said he had earned his leisure. Up until the time he retired, at the age of sixty-five, he had been the senior trust officer at the conservative old Fifth Avenue Bank, a position involving high confidentiality and heavy responsibilities. We never dared ask him about his work, nor did he ever volunteer any information concerning it; perhaps he was concerned that he might inadvertently reveal the value of a client's estate, or that a chance remark of his could give cause for scandal, which, like so many New Yorkers of his generation, he feared more than the Last Judgment. Or maybe he was just secretive by nature. In any case, it always struck me that he was paid extremely well for someone who actually kept "bankers hours," and denied himself nothing.

After he retired, our manner of living changed not at all. I wondered about that at the time, and it wasn't until much later that I found out that over the years he had made one shrewd investment after another, the returns on which amounted to considerably more than his salary at the bank.

Maybe he did earn his leisure, but I never understood how he could spend so much time just sitting. This is not to say that he took no interest in world or familial affairs: he was as well informed on the state of the nation as newspapers and periodicals could make him, and showed an uncanny aptitude for knowing everything that went on in his household. We all learned early in life that it was far wiser to observe to the letter his rules and regulations than to hope he would be unaware of any infringement of them. It was simply easier to conform than not.

I can't say we were unhappy, though; those months in East Quogue—about which I am prone to sound nostalgic—were delightful, at least up to the summer of 1916. That year, and it turned out to be our last one there, things were different. First of all, there weren't so many of us: Carrie and her family were in Bar Harbor with Dr. John Pelham's family, and Tom and Will were with us only on weekends. They were not yet married, but both were working hard in their law offices. Secondly, we no longer had our secluded point of land to ourselves. An enormously pretentious brick house had been built fairly close to our old-fashioned verandahed retreat, separated from us only by the croquet lawn and the tennis court.

"Nouveaux riches," sniffed Alfred's Ann as we sat in the rocking chairs after dinner that first night. "Only someone who has made a great deal of money in trade would build such a monstrosity." She smoothed the pleats in her exquisitely tailored linen dress as she turned to look out over the water.

I saw Rose grimace, and knew she was wondering how we would manage to get along in the same house with Ann for a month. Alfred had been forced to beg Mamma to invite his wife and children for a visit, until they were scheduled to go on to the Kittredge estate in Newport. As a matter of fact, it worked out perfectly well; Ann made no special demands on the household and conformed to all the rules. Since she had no nurse to help her, her days were pretty well taken up looking after the two little boys, then aged three and four. We really didn't see much of her, as she spent long hours on the beach while the children played, or else took them to pick whatever berries were ripening. When she left, it was almost as if she had never been there at all.

The main trouble with the big brick house was that it still looked raw, unfinished. Years later, when I was visiting friends in Southampton, they kindly drove me over to East Quogue to revisit the scenes of my childhood. By that time mature shrubbery and artful foundation plantings had so softened and improved the appearance of the house as to render it almost attractive. We never did find out what the owner did for a living, in trade or otherwise. He was a Mr. Hollins, large, ruddy, and self-assured. His wife, aside from a tendency to overdress, seemed acceptable enough.

They entertained almost constantly; it was, Rose said, as if they were running a perpetual house party. Of course, their guests required amusing, and it seemed only natural that we should offer them the use of our tennis court since theirs was still under construction. In this way Rose and I became acquainted with the two daughters of the house.

Over the past forty years I have often wondered what my sister's life would have been like if Mrs. Hollins' nephew hadn't been sent out to East Quogue to build up his strength after a prolonged illness, a severe form of bronchitis, I believe. But come he did. We met him one afternoon when several of us were gathered in the gazebo after playing tennis. We were sitting there, sipping cold, minted lemonade and enjoying the fragrance of the phlox and verbena when the younger Hollins girl came across the lawn accompanied by the latest visitor. I have never, before or since, actually seen a person fall in love, but on that warm, sunny afternoon, when the whole world seemed too languid for any emotion at all, I watched Rose do it. I couldn't really blame her; in spite of his pallor Jack Egerton was incredibly handsome. His black hair and dark eyes emphasized his pale complexion, and his tall, slender frame definitely needed filling out—but even so . . .

Perhaps it was his smile, or the look of intense interest while he listened to you, or the way his long-lashed eyes lit up as if he understood better than anyone else present the point you were making—I just don't know. In any case, during the next weeks he charmed us all, all but Papa, that is. Mamma was most favorably impressed; she had high praise for his deferential, quiet good manners (I noticed he was particularly polite to older people) and more than once intimated that Will and Tom might do worse than to emulate him.

Rose looked lovelier than ever that summer. Now that I think of it, she was always at her best in warm weather; in winter her delicate features would sometimes take on a pinched look. But that July there was an absolute glow about her; her eyes seemed to be a deeper blue, her hair a brighter gold—even her voice developed a new resonance. She wore clothes well, too; even the rather stodgy and unattractive styles of 1916 were becoming to her, and the pastel shades she loved only emphasized her flowerlike beauty. Someone, I forget who, said she always looked like a summer morning.

I remember one dress in particular that she saved for the warmest afternoons, a printed voile, with small blue flowers of some sort on a creamy background. The moderately low neckline and the short sleeves were edged with narrow bands of grosgrain ribbon of a darker blue, and a sash of the same ribbon, only wider, fitted snugly around her small waist. When she put on her wide-brimmed light-straw hat and set out for a stroll with Jack Egerton she looked for all the world as if she were off to a garden party.

She and Jack were together as much as propriety would allow, playing tennis or croquet, walking on the beach, sailing with Tom and Will on the weekends, or simply sitting on the verandah. I sensed my father's disapproval, but I doubt that Rose did. I think he was brooding because he knew so little about the young man. Egerton was reticent about his personal affairs, and aside from one casual remark about how much he would loathe returning to the hot, deserted city, he told us nothing about his family, his background, or what he did for a living. And of course we couldn't ask. I was on the point of warning Rose that he really was an unknown quantity when his visit ended, either because his health was restored, or because he had worn out his welcome in the Hollins menage. I don't know. But I do know, very definitely, that Papa disliked him: as I passed my parents' bedroom door on my way to bed the night Jack came over to say goodbye, I overheard Papa's voice.

"Well, let that be the end of it. Rose was seeing entirely too much of that young man—he's too damn handsome for his own good."

I did not hear Mamma's reply, if there was one. She was a firm believer in "least said, soonest mended," and did, I am sure, avoid a good many arguments that way.

The rest of the summer slipped away. Active mornings, lazy afternoons, and quiet evenings followed one after the other as they did every year in East Quogue. I cannot say that we frittered away our time during those fragrant, sun-filled summers, but we certainly did not do anything useful. Year after year it was the same: the months out there were set aside for pleasure, and no one was ever in a hurry to return to the city. Summer's lease was indeed too short.

That year, however, I was quite ready to go back, even before the season drew to a close. I had what used to be called "an understanding" with Ben Hastings and hadn't seen him since June. Our engagement would be announced in October, and we planned an April wedding. Rose was to be my maid of honor. I think my parents would have been happier if I had accepted Ned Cochrane when he proposed, but they liked Ben well enough, and although they may have thought him a bit dashing they had to admit that he was considered quite a catch. The Hastings were an old and respected Gramercy Park family—even Papa couldn't find fault with them—comfortably off, but not nearly as rich as the Cochranes. I wonder now if that had something to do with Papa's request that I reconsider.

Anyway, I was sitting in the gazebo that last day, resting after helping with the packing and feeling a little annoyed at Rose for not doing her share. After breakfast she said she wanted to do a last-minute errand in the village, and slipped out before anyone could ask her about it. I was happy, though, at the prospect of seeing Ben in two days' time; he had written that he had booked a table at Delmonico's for dinner, and that afterward we would see young John Barrymore in *Dr. Jekyll and Mr. Hyde*. I was wondering which dress I would wear, or whether I would have time to buy a new one, when Katie came running across the lawn to tell me that no one could find Miss Rose and that my mother was hysterical.

2

I don't think my parents ever fully recovered from the shock of Rose's disappearance. Mamma was in bed for days after it happened, heavily sedated; my father withdrew into himself, speaking only when necessary. Naturally our return to New York was postponed until Mamma was able to travel, and the days dragged on as if we were going through a period of endless mourning.

The brick house next door was shuttered and closed up for the season; I don't know where the Hollins family went; we never saw or heard from them again. Thinking that Rose might have gone off with Jack Egerton, I asked Papa to call on Mrs. Hollins before they left to see if we could get in touch with her nephew, but he said that would be demeaning. And besides, he went on, we weren't at all sure that Rose had eloped with him. I was almost sure, and I think he was, too, but I knew better than to try to convince him to do anything that would, in his eyes, constitute a loss of face.

One by one the other summer houses in East Quogue were left empty, boats were put away, awnings taken down, bath houses locked up, and all the paraphernalia of summer disappeared, adding to our already heightened sense of desolation. If I hadn't been so worried and unhappy I probably would have enjoyed the gradual approach of autumn in those quiet surroundings, but as it was I was too miserable to appreciate beauty in any form. And little things, such as not having the proper clothes for the cooler weather, bothered me. I was not sleeping well, either; at night, long after the rest of the household was quiet, I would lie awake, one moment worried sick about Rose and the next furious at her for causing such misery.

"Poor little thing—she's so young—so vulnerable," I would say to myself, and then, "She's selfish—she'd no right—she never gave a thought to anyone but herself. Why couldn't she have told us, left a note? Why doesn't she send word? I could kill her—"

Kill her! Mamma kept insisting, in her lucid moments, that Rose was already dead, and then she would cry and moan until the nurse sedated her again. Goodness knows how her system ever tolerated all that laudanum.

And then it was suddenly over, at least the not-knowing part was over. At the end of the third week, Alfred telephoned, saying he had heard from Rose, that she had married Jack Egerton, and that she was going out west to live with him. She didn't say where in the west, but she wanted him, Alfred, to break the news to Mamma and Papa. That was all. It was so like Rose to be indirect, to use Alfred that way. She could just as easily have phoned us, but I guess she was afraid of Papa. But perhaps I am being unfair to her;

after all, all of us were well versed in methods of avoiding scenes and confrontations.

Of course, I was relieved that she was safe, but I was also angry, and the feeling persisted for some time after we were back in the Sixty-fifth Street house. It wasn't too long, though, before I realized that I really did not care very much if I never saw Rose again. I can't imagine how this happened, but that's the way I felt. Not so my parents; they kept hoping against hope that she would return and that somehow, miraculously, all would be as it had been before the appearance of Jack Egerton.

She did return eventually, but in the meantime the world did not stand still, nor was there much to be happy about. America entered the war in Europe, and most of the young men were called up or volunteered. Tom and Will and Ben Hastings were among the first to go, and naturally my wedding was postponed. My brothers returned unscathed after the armistice, but Ben was listed as missing in the battle of Château-Thierry. I found I had no aptitude for knitting, rolling bandages, or any other kind of volunteer work, so rather than idle away the miserable days, I activated my teaching certificate and went to work instructing eighth-graders in the grammer school on the corner of Sixty-eighth Street and Lexington, opposite the school for deaf children. Little did I think then that I was to go on teaching at various levels for thirty years or more.

Even after the war was over, after Tom and Will were married, and I was alone in the big brownstone house with my parents I kept alive the hope that Ben would be found in some hospital in France slightly, only slightly wounded. Hope—it was all I had. That, and the fact that I was formally engaged to Ben, prevented me from going about with Ned Cochrane. Dear Ned! He was, Tom used to say, as faithful as old dog Tray. He came back from overseas looking lean, but well, and making light of the shrapnel wound in his right leg. It bothered him hardly at all, he told us, just a twinge or two in damp weather.

"The doctors said I was most fortunate," he said one day in reply to a question of Mamma's. "Another inch one way or the other and I'd have had a permanent limp. No, really, I'm fine."

Then turning away from her, he asked Papa what he thought about the League of Nations. It was typical of Ned to steer the conversation away from himself, and while Papa carried on about President Wilson and I helped Mamma with the tea things I had a sudden mental picture of Ned sitting in his office listening to a client unburdening himself. There was an indefinable quality about him that inspired confidence and trust—I suppose that was one reason why he was so successful in his law firm and why he had been made a partner while he was still quite young.

It was probably a combination of things that made people trust him—his frank, open countenance, his deferential (but by no means obsequious) manner, his deep, well-modulated voice, and his generally pleasing appearance. He was tall, well above average height, and had a habit of leaning forward, toward one, during a conversation, as he gave his full attention to whatever was being said. He had a surprisingly boyish laugh, which I suspect was one of the things that endeared him to Mamma. He would call from time to time, generally on a Sunday afternoon, and entertain us for an hour or so with the lighter side of the legal profession (at least he made it seem as if the law had a lighter side). I was always glad to see him, but I was equally glad that he did not press his suit.

Then one day in the spring of 1920 I received a note from his mother asking me to have tea with her some afternoon after school. I had been to two or three formal parties at the Cochrane house, down on Forty-ninth Street near Park, and had admired its spaciousness, if not its furnishings. A double brownstone, nearly twice the size of ours, it gave an immediate impression of solidity and wealth with its wide marble entrance hall and formal reception rooms. Without question, everything was beautifully maintained by an efficient staff; only charm and comfort were lacking. Perhaps the furniture had to be massive because of the size of the rooms, but did it all have to be dark and gloomy and cruelly carved? The predominant colors were brown and dark red, maroon, I guess, which remained dull even in lamplight.

I always thought Mrs. Cochrane, a delicate, blond woman, looked out of place in those surroundings; the sunny colors of Florida, where she spent part of every winter, must have suited her far better. She was considered to be an accomplished hostess, and a clever person, but clever or not she made a mistake, a bad mistake, in undertaking to plead Ned's cause. All I could think of that afternoon as I sat in her formal sitting room sipping my tea was what a sorry role any matchmaker plays. Even though I realized that she had only Ned's happiness at heart, I was extremely uncomfortable. In fact, her arguments not only embarrassed me, but made me feel antagonistic toward her.

"Ned's father left us both well off, Grace; you would want for nothing, my dear. And my boy worships the

27

ground you walk on—not too many women have that, you know."

"But, Mrs. Cochrane—"

"This house is so large that the three of us would have no trouble living comfortably without interfering with each other, and there's the summer place in Remsenberg. And don't you think, Grace, that you ought to realize that Ben Hastings will not be coming back? It's been so long, and you are not getting any younger, you know. Also, I'm sure you are aware that at least two young women of your acquaintance have been pursuing Ned rather obviously—"

And on and on it went. I just kept repeating that I was not ready to marry—it seemed the politic thing to say—and finally took my leave, but not before she clasped my hand in both of hers and assured me that neither she nor Ned would give up hope. As I rode uptown on the Lexington Avenue trolley, I kept hearing her words, "Neither Ned nor I, my dear, neither Ned nor I, my dear—" over and over again, like a refrain.

Mrs. Cochrane had a soft, cultured voice, very pleasant to the ear, and I am at a loss to know why I regarded her last remark as threatening. I have already mentioned that I dislike being pushed into anything— maybe that was it. She was right about Adelaide Graham and Kitty Manville, though; everyone in New York knew they had been after Ned for years. But live in the same house as Mrs. Cochrane? Impossible.

Mamma once told me that Leila Cochrane had been known years ago as one of the most beautiful women in the city, and I could well believe it. She must have been over fifty at the time I speak of, but with her unlined face, her abundant light blond hair, and her slim figure, she could have passed for a woman in her thirties. Only her hands would have given her away; they were deformed by arthritis, not too badly then, but they would gradually degenerate into the hands of a crone. I was afraid of the soft voice and the claw.

Of course I didn't mention the visit to Ned, and I am reasonably sure his mother said nothing about it. I am also sure that she counted on my silence; in any case, there was no change in Ned's behavior that I could see. He still came to tea most Sundays, and about once a month Mamma invited him to dinner. As for me, nothing seemed to matter very much. I drifted through that spring of 1920 as I had been drifting ever since we heard that Ben was missing, not caring very much about anything. No, that isn't right; I did care about my students. I enjoyed teaching, and I knew I was doing it well. Thank God I had it to do. Without it I might have lapsed into depression or melancholy or something equally awful.

The summers were particularly trying; each year my parents and I went north to the Berkshires or the Adirondacks for July and August (no one ever mentioned East Quogue), and although the hotels we stayed at were first-class and the surrounding scenery left nothing to be desired, the enforced idleness nearly drove me crazy. Three years of that were enough, I decided. So when in April Papa started making plans for a summer in the White Mountains of New Hampshire, I said I wanted to stay in the city and take some courses toward a master's degree.

My father was completely opposed to the idea; he simply would not face the fact that by that time I was twenty-five years old and well beyond the realm of parental jurisdiction. Mamma understood the situation much better than he did, and so, of course, did Ned, who was there for tea when I made my announcement.

"But why," Papa expostulated, "would she want to stay in the hot city, sitting in dusty classrooms listening to some dullard carry on about Chaucer and Shakespeare and those fellows by the hour when she could be up in the mountains building up her strength for next winter?"

"But, Papa, my health has never been better—"

"And another thing: you'd be all alone at night in this big house—anything might happen—thieves, murderers, adventurers! I do not like it! And what will people say if we go off and leave a young girl unchaperoned?"

"You forget, James," Mamma said quietly, "the maids will be here. It's not the way it used to be before we went to hotels. They have no other homes, you know."

I noticed how carefully she avoided any mention of East Quogue, but even so, Papa's face fell and his shoulders drooped as he turned away from us and stood looking out the window. Fortunately Carrie chose that moment to arrive with two of her "brood," and their noisy chatter about new roller skates diverted him temporarily.

"Of course you must do it, Grace," Carrie said when I told her what I had in mind. "And don't stop with the master's; go on to the doctorate. You always loved going to school, and I can see that you still do. Goodness knows, I'd love to go back myself, but that will have to wait until the children are older. Even then, I don't suppose my John will take kindly to the idea. But you, you're a free agent, and have a right to the life you want."

Poor Carrie! She never had a chance to find out what

she could do with her life. In spite of all the specialists Dr. John Pelham brought in, she died in 1925 of complications resulting from diabetes. They didn't know as much about the disease then as they do now. But her support of my proposal tipped the balance, and on the first of July I found myself alone in a house I hardly recognized. Rugs and carpets (except those on the stairs, which were nailed down) were taken up and sent out to be cleaned and stored for the summer, exposing the unfamiliar, beautiful parquet floors. Pictures, chandeliers, tables, and chairs were shrouded in dust sheets, and even the mantelpieces were covered with some sort of runners. The maids had orders to clean, scrub, and polish everything in sight, and to serve me my meals on the drop-leaf table in the front parlor, where one chair and one lamp had been left unswathed. My own room, except for the removal of the rug, had not been touched, and since I had my books, my desk, and a comfortable chaise longue in there, I really had no need of the rest of the house.

I didn't feel exactly uneasy, but perhaps I was a bit nervous, because I know I closed the door to my parents' bedroom so that I wouldn't see the stripped beds. Also, I took to locking my door at night, something I had never done in the past, and putting a chair against the bathroom door, which could be locked only from the other side. The first few nights I kept hearing noises I could not identify, and did not sleep well. This led me to ask Dr. Bronson for a mild sleeping pill, and I had no further trouble. (He told me years later he had given me a placebo; he hasn't changed his thinking in that respect.)

The maids and I saw very little of each other; once in a while I would hear them talking or laughing or meet one of them on the stairs, but that was about all. After the summer courses started at NYU, I found it easier to have breakfast and lunch at the university cafeteria or in a nearby restaurant with other graduate students. Sometimes, if I had work to do in the library, I stayed out for dinner as well. Occasionally I accepted an invitation to dine with Ned. I knew Mrs. Cochrane had gone to Remsenberg for the summer, so there was no danger of her reading more into these acceptances than was actually there. Ned spent his weekends with her, leaving the city on Friday afternoon and not returning until Monday morning, when he went straight to the office from the train.

I had thought at first that the weekends might be troublesome—I mean, that I might be lonely—but I was far too busy. Since the courses I had elected involved heavy reading and extensive research, the empty weekends turned out to be a blessing, but even so, toward the end of the summer session I was up late every night completing term papers and studying for the final examinations. I was beginning to feel tired, to long for a few days with nothing in the world to do, and toyed with the idea of joining my parents in the mountains for the last week in August. Then when I thought of the packing, the long train ride, and the artificial life at the end of it, I decided to stay put and regroup my forces in the emptiness of the city house.

New York was in the midst of a late summer heat wave that week, with the thermometer reaching one hundred degrees in the daytime and not dropping below ninety at night. The papers were full of reports of heat prostrations, warnings about overexertion, and frequent drownings at the crowded beaches. I suppose I could have felt depressed and sorry for myself, but strangely enough I was quite content. The high-ceilinged rooms of the old house, especially the ones facing north, stayed relatively cool, so I was reasonably comfortable as I sat reading in the window of the front parlor, sipping the iced drinks Cook sent up to me several times a day. Also, I was at peace with myself: I had a tremendous sense of satisfaction, almost of euphoria, of having done a good job. I knew I had done well in my courses, and as the tiredness receded I began to dwell with enthusiasm on next summer's work. When I found myself feeling a bit annoyed that the list of course offerings would not be available until later in the year, I knew I had chosen the right discipline, and that there was a good chance of my carving out a successful academic career for myself.

I don't want to give the impression that I was completely happy; I wasn't, but I knew I could not afford to think about Ben or to worry about Rose if I wanted to stay rational. As I said earlier, I had reached the point where I didn't really care whether I ever saw my sister again, but that did not prevent me from wondering, every so often, about her well-being. As for Ben, I knew that his parents kept in constant touch with the military authorities, the Red Cross, and other government agencies in their search for news of him, and since Mr. Hastings was known to have a number of friends in high places it seemed to me that the utmost was being done. There was nothing to be gained by my allowing myself the luxury of yearning for him, and one evening I went so far as to remove the engagement ring he had given me from my finger and put it away in my jewelry box; it seemed to have lost its meaning.

In a way, I buried Rose and Ben, buried them in separate boxes in the back of my mind. I suppose a modern psychiatrist would have urged me to talk about them to avoid all that repression, which my stiff, proper, Victorian upbringing would not permit.

The relative solitude of that hot week at the end of August was enjoyable, but only up to a point. By Thursday I was ready, in spite of the heat, to go abroad, as Mamma would say, even if she was merely going over to the florist on Third Avenue or down to Bloomingdale's to buy a pair of gloves. School would reopen the Monday after Labor Day, and I needed a few dark cotton dresses to see me through September. I was about to set out for an especially nice little shop on Sixty-second Street when Ned phoned and asked me to have dinner with him.

"Even in this heat, Grace, you need to get out," he insisted. "You've incarcerated yourself for most of the summer with your books and papers—"

"I'd love it, Ned. Will you call for me? About seven?"

I thought if I were lucky I might be able to find a fall dinner dress in addition to the utilitarian cottons— nothing fancy, just something new that I could wear that night.

When I told Maggie to let Cook know I would not dine at home, her face fell.

"Dear, oh dear! And Cook's just after spendin' the mornin' making the chicken in aspic you favor so! She'll be that disappointed, Miss Grace," she wailed.

Cook becomes upset all too easily, I thought, remembering how careful Mamma always was in the way she handled her. I am not sure how long this had been going on—years and years, I guess. Keeping Cook happy was just one of the things we did in that house; it was a fixed rule.

In the end it was decided that there was plenty of chicken in aspic if Mr. Ned would like to stay in for dinner, and that there would be shrimp cocktail first and a macédoine of fruit for dessert. And of course the meal would be served in the dining room. At least that's what we agreed on, but I remember thinking as I walked down Lexington Avenue that Cook would embellish the menu as she saw fit. She would probably send up a few delicious little canapes delicately arranged on a lace doily to accompany our sherry; a basket of feather-light rolls would appear with the aspic; a marinated vegetable of some sort would be served as a side dish, and heaven only knew what confection would supplement the macédoine. A simple, unadorned meal for a guest, especially a male guest, was not only an impossibility, it was virtually anathema. Anyway, I knew Ned would love it.

It was not a good day for trying on dresses; the little shop, in spite of drawn shades and whirring fans, was brutally hot. Perspiration dripped from my forehead and fabrics clung to my skin. I persisted only because I found exactly what I wanted: three sensible dark cottons and a soft, silk paisley. Skirts were an awkward length in 1920, mid-calf, I think they called it, and even slender women like me had to be careful to avoid that extra inch, or even half-inch, that would give the costume a bedraggled look. The shorter skirts that came in a few years later were far easier to wear, at least for those of us who had good legs.

The dresses I bought that day all featured the natural waistline and self-covered buttons; the sleeves of the ones for school were all three-quarter length, finished off with narrow satin binding. The silk paisley, though, had long, full sleeves with tight cuffs at the wrists. I always felt more elegantly dressed if I wore long sleeves, but for school the shorter ones were more practical. I tried on one dress in a style that was just then coming in, with the waistline down around the hips, but it didn't have a trim look, so I rejected it in spite of the shopowner's warning that all dresses would be of that cut in the near future. After promising to return on a cooler day for another look, I left the shop, exhausted, but with a sense of accomplishment.

The heat of the sidewalk penetrated the thin soles of my shoes, and when I crossed the street my heels sank into its tarry surface. It was all a bit eerie; the avenue was deserted, and the sun that had baked the city for days had disappeared, leaving behind a heavy grayness and no relief from the heat. No, "eerie" is not the right word; "ominous" is better. I shivered a little as I stood at the top of the stoop waiting for someone to answer the door. (Generally I used my key, but I had so many packages that day that I couldn't get at my purse.)

"Oh, Miss Grace, dear, you look worn out, you do," Katie cried as she took my boxes. "Sit you down, I'll bring you some iced tea, good and cold." And she was off in a flurry.

"I must be a sight," I thought, "if Katie noticed. It's a good thing she didn't see me shiver, or she would have warned me that someone was walking over my grave."

I recovered quickly, however, and by half-past six, rested, bathed, and dressed in a cool georgette dress from the previous summer, I was ready for a pleasant evening with my old friend. Sometimes things have a way of working out: at a few minutes before seven I heard the first loud claps of thunder, and by the time Ned's taxi drew up in front of the house heavy rain was beating down.

"Grace, you are wonderful, you really are!" he exclaimed as he poured the sherry. "Who else could have known that this would be no night to be ducking in and out of cabs and restaurants?"

He laughed when I explained the real reason we were dining at home and said he understood the situation perfectly.

"You've seen the couple we have, haven't you? Even my mother doesn't dare cross Mrs. Brady. And the maids and Brady hop to it when she gives an order. But she's a good soul underneath the bossiness, and a marvelous cook. She loves the summers in Remsenberg because she can get so many different kinds of seafood right from the fisherman, with whom she bargains fiercely. And would you believe it, she insists on taking an extra trunk out there every summer, filled with her special pots and pans!"

We were laughing over one of my favorite "Cook" stories when dinner was announced—in fact we laughed a good deal that evening. I remember Ned's telling me about an aged and ever so respectable client of his who was suddenly seized with the desire to visit the house in which he had lived as a child, and set out to do so. What he didn't realize was that the building (a brownstone very like ours) had been made over into a rooming house. He went confidently up the stairs to his old bedroom, woke its occupant from a sound sleep, and narrowly escaped being arrested for trespassing, unlawful entry, and half a dozen other things.

And Ned listened with genuine interest while I recalled some of the lighter moments of my academic summer. He surprised me, too, by saying that if it hadn't been ordained that he follow in his father's footsteps and take up the law he would have chosen to become a professor of literature. I refrained from saying that he should have been free to make the choice, but Ned was too fine a person for me to hurt any more than I already had. And he did seem happy enough in the legal world, although I wonder now if like so many of us of that generation he wasn't merely making the best of things, almost relinquishing any personal control of his life. But would he have been any better off if he had thrown over the traces, any happier? Look at Rose . . . I think that, in the end, those of us who conformed, at least outwardly, came off better, but, then, did we miss something?

When Ned was preparing to leave shortly after ten o'clock the rain had stopped and the air felt slightly cooler; we could still hear occasional thunder in the distance, which we thought meant the storm was on its way out to sea.

"I don't want the evening to end," he said as I went to the door with him—I wondered then if he had noticed the absence of Ben Hasting's ring. "Come, walk me to the corner, Grace, and I'll walk you back. The air will do you good—"

He broke off. We both heard the sound of a key being fitted into the lock at the same instant. A moment later the knob turned and the door was pushed slowly inward. I screamed, I know, as Ned thrust me behind him and flung the door wide open. A dark figure bolted down the steps, and as Ned raced after it, a terrific clap of thunder announced that the storm had returned to the city.

C H A P T E R

3

Ned was to laugh later at the sight that met his eyes when he returned, wet and exhausted, from a fruitless chase.

"I'll never forget it, Grace," he would say, "four women huddled together in the front hall armed with pokers, frying pans, and toasting forks! If the intruder had ever been confronted with that he would have thrown in the towel without a murmur."

It didn't seem funny at the time. Cook, the maids, and I were so thoroughly terrified that Ned said he would stay overnight and sleep on the parlor sofa if we could find him some dry clothes. Katie made a frightened Maggie go with her to dig out some old summer things that Alfred had left behind, and after Ned had changed (decorously, in the back parlor), the two maids carried his wet suit down to the kitchen to press it dry.

"Did you see his face, Ned," I asked when we were alone.

"I didn't get a good look at him at all, Grace—"

"Can we be sure it was a man?"

"Almost positively, from the way he ran, from the sound of his shoes on pavement, and from what I could see of his build. And I don't think a woman could have leapt down the stoop that fast—it was someone with very long legs."

"All I saw was a dark shape. And then there was the key—Ned, who could have a key?"

"Excuse me, Miss Grace," Katie said from the doorway. "Cook sent up some warm milk. She said it would be better for the both of you than coffee at this hour."

"Thank you, Katie, and thank Cook for her thoughtfulness."

Thoughtfulness, indeed! With the first sip I realized that a good dollop of Irish whiskey had been added—Cook's cure-all, we used to call it.

Ned and I sat up until nearly midnight, but the only decision we reached was that we postpone calling the police until the morning. It seemed like the right thing to do, because we were both tired out, and if a detective or a policeman were summoned then, we were afraid we'd be up for the rest of the night. As it was, perhaps thanks to the fortified milk, or to Ned's presence downstairs, I slept as soundly as if nothing had happened.

I guess Ned did, too, because when I went downstairs the next morning I overheard him teasing Cook about her "sleeping potion," a cheerful start to what turned out to be a most trying day.

The two policemen who came over from the Sixty-seventh Street Station House in answer to our call were polite enough and anxious to help, but since neither of us could describe the intruder in any detail there wasn't much they could do except to recommend

that we have the locks changed and call them immediately if it happened again.

"Grace, look here," Ned said after they left, "try to
think who has keys to the house: your parents, of
course, and you—do the maids have any?"

"Yes, Cook has one, and the other two borrow it
when necessary. But, Ned, they were in the house
with us, and Mamma and Papa are away."

"We'll have to make up a list of all possible key
holders and see that they're all accounted for; someone
who should not have one does. If we find out which
one is missing—"

"But I have no idea whether the boys and Carrie
kept theirs when they were married or not. And
Rose—I just don't know. We all had two keys, one for
the front door and one for the areaway, just for the
iron door, the grating. We've never bothered with the
inside, wooden one. Oh, dear, this isn't getting us
anyplace, Ned. When the locksmith comes I'll order
four sets of keys: one for each of my parents, one for
Cook, and one for me. The others won't need any
now."

"What about the back door, from the kitchen into
the yard?" he asked. "Don't you have a key for that?"

"No, there's never been one. No one ever comes in
that way, and at night it's bolted on the inside. Cook
sees to it."

We left it at that. Ned waited until the locksmith had
finished his work and then left, saying he would be in
the office for a few hours before catching the train for
Remsenberg and that I was to call him there if I needed
him. He tried to persuade me to go out to Long Island
with him, but I couldn't face the thought of a weekend
with Mrs. Cochrane. She would, I was sure, jump to
the conclusion that I had accepted Ned, in which case

everything would be embarrassing. And, I thought, if she didn't reach that conclusion, she might try to bring it about. Besides, I was afraid Cook would take it amiss if I left just then.

Looking back on that weekend, I can honestly say that it was one of the worst I have ever spent: I don't think I slept more than two or three hours on Friday or Saturday night, even though I took one of Dr. Bronson's pills. I purposely tried to wear myself out during the day by helping the maids get the house ready for my parents' return on Monday. I made beds, unrolled carpets, removed dust covers, relined dresser drawers, and so on. I must have run up and down the stairs dozens of times, I know, because the backs of my legs began to ache. But still I could not sleep.

I was worried, too, about alarming my mother and father with the tale of the intruder; I wasn't sure about Papa's reaction, but I knew Mamma would be frightened half to death. By Sunday afternoon I had decided to say nothing, and to explain the new locks by telling them that the old ones were worn to the point where they would no longer engage the key. I would be deceiving them, I knew, but I felt strongly that the deception was necessary. I alerted the maids to my plan, and all three agreed it would be wise not to upset the old couple.

"I'll just say that the lock broke, should anybody ask me," Katie said.

"And you'll say nothing unless someone does ask you," Cook said sternly. "And Maggie, my girl, you can stop taking the toasting fork to bed with you; you'll do yourself an injury, you will—" and she broke off to tend the pot she had simmering on the stove. I knew without asking that she was preparing Papa's favorite beef and barley soup, always made a day in advance so that the flavor would "come out."

"Miss Grace," she called as I turned to leave, "you need to rest. Go now, and get off your feet, and I'll send your tea up to you."

I did rest for a while on the chaise longue, and then went out to mail a note to Ned, apprising him of my small deception. It was a lovely late summer day, and despite my tired legs I decided to walk over to the park. As I approached Fifth Avenue my eyes were drawn, as they so often were, to the enormous granite mansion John Jacob Astor had built at the end of the last century on the corner of Sixty-fifth and Fifth. The very bulk of the structure both fascinated and repelled me; it seemed entirely too large to be a home, and too small to be a castle. Although it was far from being aesthetically pleasing, it did have some interesting and unusual architectural details: graceful columns rose on either side of a triple window on the first floor; elaborate scrolls and finials surmounted smaller, third-floor windows, creating the effect of miniature temples, and strangely enough, the windows on the intervening second floor were absolutely unadorned, standing out in stark contrast to those above and below. One could but wonder whether the inner grandeur (or lack of it) corresponded to what was visible to the outside world. Was that second story as empty as its windows? Was it uncarpeted, unlit, unused, an area of cold space, past which the inhabitants hurried on their way up from the brilliantly lighted, mirrored luxury of the public rooms on the first floor to the jewelled boudoirs behind the temple windows? And, I wondered, how did Cook, Maggie, and Katie feel every time they made their way up past our empty fourth floor where Carrie and the boys had lived?

Emptiness also existed between the Astor house and the outside world: as I lowered my glance I saw the black iron railing that separated the sidewalk from what we used to call "the moat," but what was really an enormous areaway running all along the Sixty-fifth Street side of the house and up to the magnificent front entrance on Fifth Avenue. There were barred windows opening onto this moat below the street level, and once in a while we would catch a glimpse of what appeared to be an army of servants moving about inside.

That Sunday, however, the enormous house had the dreary, vacant look of so many of the winter houses of wealthy New Yorkers in summer, standing idly in the late afternoon sun, waiting for the festivities of "the season" to commence. I mused over the whereabouts of its occupants; were they in an equally grand establishment in Newport, or roughing it in a luxurious Adirondack lodge? Or relaxing on the decks of a private yacht? Did they have sisters who ran away, fiancés who disappeared in France? Did strangers procure keys to their front doors and try to intrude?

This train of thought was abruptly interrupted: a man who turned into the side street from Fifth Avenue stopped suddenly, grasped the black iron railing as if to keep from falling, and stood still. It looked to me (from my side of the street) as if he were coughing—at least his shoulders were shaking. He wasn't shabbily dressed like one of the drunkards or vagrants we occasionally saw, so I thought he might have been taken ill. I was looking around to see if I could find someone to help him when he righted himself and set off in the direction of Madison Avenue. I did not see his face, which he kept turned toward the Astor house, but there was something slightly familiar about his walk—was it Ben who had that long stride?

I crossed over into the park and strolled past the old Arsenal up to Donkey Hill, where I found a quiet bench in the shade. The paths were almost deserted; a few children went by on roller skates, an elderly man threw bread crumbs to the pigeons, a young couple tried patiently to teach a little boy how to ride a tricycle, and every once in a while I could hear the tired roar of one of the zoo's old lions. The other New York, I thought, the one the very rich never knew, for all their proximity to the scene.

I walked home, feeling refreshed and composed, ready for whatever delicious food Cook had decided would be good for me, and reasonably sure that I would sleep well that night. I was also sure that I would have no problem sleeping after my parents returned, although it occurred to me that their presence in the house really meant very little in the way of protection. Papa would hear nothing, and Mamma would faint dead away at the first sign of trouble. Why was it, then, that I felt sure of feeling safe once they came back? It made no sense then, and it makes none now, but that's how I felt at the time.

To my surprise, my brother Alfred was in the front parlor when I got home. He generally spent the latter part of August with Ann and her parents in Newport, returning only at the end of the Labor Day weekend. The senior Kittredges more or less demanded his presence at their end-of-summer festivities, ostensibly to give him "a good rest," but actually, I always thought, to present a solid family front to the world in which they moved. They were very much concerned with publicity (the right kind, of course), too, and saw to it

that photographs of Alfred, Ann, and the two boys appeared on the society pages of the appropriate
periodicals and papers. I still have one of those pictures, showing Ann, looking very beautiful and elegant, smiling down at Charles and Francis, and Alfred
with a serious, slightly puzzled expression standing
beside her—altogether a charming group, worthy of
the Kittredge clan.

My brother was generally considered handsome, but
conservatively so. What I mean is that he did not stand
out in a crowd. I guess he had what people used to call
"pleasant good looks." That Sunday afternoon, however, his physical appearance startled me. He had always been on the thin side, and his rather long face
had never been full; that day it looked almost gaunt.
His light-colored hair had begun to recede a bit from
his forehead, thus adding years to his age. He had a
glass of whiskey in his hand, and the decanter was on
the little table next to his chair.

"Grace!" he cried, striding across the room toward
me. "Maggie said you'd be right back, so I waited. I
must talk to you—"

"Alfred, how good to see you! Will you stay and
have dinner with me? Cook would love it."

"I don't know. Maybe. Look, Grace, I need help.
Ann has—"

"Miss Grace, will Mr. Alfred be staying for dinner?
Cook would like to know." Maggie stood beaming in
the doorway. Alfred nodded, rather distractedly, and
she left, humming some Irish song to herself.

My brother pulled a chair up to the sofa where I sat
and began to talk in a voice scarcely above a whisper.

"Alfred, I can hardly hear you! What on earth is the
matter? Why are you in the city—isn't this your vaca-

tion? I thought you were in Newport with the Kittredges."

"What I said was that I am in trouble, deep trouble.
Financial. I don't know where to turn. I've borrowed
so much, the interest is killing me. You've no idea
what it's like, Grace. I lost some money in the stock
market last spring—lots of people did—and then Ann
runs up the most outrageous bills for gowns, furs,
even jewels—I can't get her to stop. When I try, her
answer is always the same: 'Oh, we'll manage somehow!' But I've reached the point where I cannot manage. I thought I could pull through, just barely, until
the firm hands out the end-of-the-year bonuses, and
then I was hit with bills from Milgrim's—some of them
over six months old! She'd saved them up."

He stared at the floor for a moment, and then got up
to pour himself another drink. That in itself was out of
character; he had always been abstemious, taking a little sherry now and then, a glass of wine at dinner, but
seldom anything stronger. No one in the family drank
very much, although my father kept an unusually
well-stocked cellar, so well stocked, in fact, that all
through the prohibition years he never ran short.

Katie came in with a plate of toasted cheese tidbits,
and I waited until she was out of earshot before speaking to the distraught man pacing the floor in front of
the empty grate.

"Alfred, sit down, here. Look, I have about five
thousand in my account. That would help, wouldn't
it? No interest, of course. Then you could pay the most
pressing of the bills at least. And Alfred, wouldn't you
consider moving to a less expensive neighborhood?
The rent on that house must be exorbitant."

"That would be over Ann's dead body," he said

47

glumly. "She'd lose face with her family, all her rich friends—"

"But you can't go on like this. You'll only go deeper into debt. Would the Kittredges help? Could they make Ann an allowance?"

"I can't ask them, Grace. Her grandmother settled an annuity on her when we were married. It gives her about a thousand a month, but that goes through her fingers like water. Of course, she does stand to inherit a fortune—"

"Do you want me to speak to Ann?"

"Hell, no. Excuse me. I mean, it would only make things worse. She'd rant and rave at me for publicizing my troubles. Thanks, Grace, but no."

Just then dinner was announced, and as we went down I whispered to him that I thought I knew a way, which I would tell him about later. Then I asked him to put on a cheerful face and eat as if he were enjoying the food, or Cook would be cross.

He managed a faint smile, and offered me his arm.

4

Alfred left early, somewhat unsteadily (he'd had two glasses of brandy after dinner, and I'm pretty sure he'd been drinking before he came to the house). As I prepared for bed and went over the events of the evening, I could no longer suppress the thought that had been in the back of my mind right along: could it have been Alfred I saw holding onto the railing of the Astor house? I couldn't remember much about that man except that he was tall, slender, and wore a dark suit. Alfred was tall, slender, and his suit was navy blue. Alfred was not coughing—but still—

He had reluctantly agreed to my suggestion that he approach Ned Cochrane the next day. He and Ned had been friends for years, so it wouldn't be like dealing with a stranger. Ned was not only wealthy, but he was also generous and compassionate, and I felt sure he would let Alfred have an unsecured loan at little or no interest. What I was not sure of was how my brother would be able to control his wife's extravagances, and unless he could do that his financial position would never be stable. Also, given his present mental and physical condition, the chances of his being able to cope well with anything at all seemed dubious. I wasn't at all happy about him and did not spend a restful night after all.

I was about to leave the house the next afternoon to meet my parents' train at Grand Central Station when Ned phoned.

"I can't talk now, Ned," I said. "I have to get down to the station—"

"Just two things, Grace. First, I have your note about the keys. I agree. Second, Alfred's OK. Don't worry. I'll drop by tomorrow evening."

Dear Ned. I thanked him and hung up.

My father and mother were tired and out of sorts after the long train trip. Mamma went straight upstairs to lie down, while Maggie unpacked for her. Papa, as I knew he would, inspected the entire house before settling down with the evening paper. He looked the picture of comfort sitting there in the large armchair, with one leg crossed over the other and spirals of smoke rising from his pipe. He was a big man, heavy without being fat, which is strange because he ate heartily at every meal and avoided all kinds of exercise. I remember thinking how well he looked that afternoon; his face was slightly tanned from his months in the mountains, making the whiteness of his mustache and carefully brushed hair stand out. He was meticulous about his dress, and even after the dusty train ride (I knew he hadn't had time to change) looked as fresh and unrumpled as if he had just come downstairs in the morning.

When he asked me to pour him a second cup of tea, I told him about the new keys. He accepted my story about the worn-out locks without any fuss, merely commenting that he thought the locksmith had charged entirely too much for such a small job.

"Grace," he said suddenly, putting the newspaper aside, "I want to talk to you about your mother. I don't like the way she's been looking lately. She tires easily, too. Now, I want her to see a doctor—not old Gillespie, he's not seeing many patients these days—but that young fellow, Bronson. I like him; he's up-and-coming, and he'll know what to do. And your job is to persuade her to see him. It won't be easy, but I want you to do it.

"And while you're at it," he went on before I could say anything, "have him give you a tonic. You're too thin—only to be expected, spending the hot weather in the city. I wish you had been with us."

"Now, James, don't fuss at Grace the moment you get home," Mamma said as she came into the parlor. "She does look a bit thinner, but I think it's becoming. She has very good bones, you know. As a matter of fact, my dear, you look prettier than ever. You don't need a tonic any more than I do."

Papa grunted and went back to his paper.

I waited until the next morning to carry out his orders, and I can still see Mamma as she sat at the breakfast table that day, all pink and white and rested, wearing one of her sprigged "morning dresses" and smelling faintly of lavender. Papa had finished his breakfast and gone up to the parlor with the *Times*, so the two of us were alone at the table. She eyed me speculatively while I told her that I thought it would be a good idea if the doctor checked her over. I carried on about how Carrie's husband insisted that his wife and children see a physician once a year, and about how careful Ann was of the health of Charles and Francis.

She listened quietly, but when I paused she sounded angry.

"Don't tell me, Grace Millerton, that your father isn't behind all this! He's been after me for months to see a doctor, and now he's enlisting you! There isn't a thing the matter with me, but I can see that I'll not have a moment's peace unless I capitulate—yes, Maggie, I will have another cup of coffee."

She would not, however, go to the doctor's office. "If he wants to see me, let him come here, Grace. And tell him not to stay too long."

Dr. Bronson did not stay too long. When he came downstairs after what must have been an extremely brief examination and saw Papa's anxious face he smiled in a reassuring manner.

"Nothing to worry about, Mr. Millerton, nothing at all. She's frail, but she's fundamentally healthy. I'll send some medicine over for a slight weakening of the heart; that should take care of things. And Grace, keep her away from coffee if you can, and don't let them make the tea too strong."

"Her heart? What's wrong with her heart?" My father sounded almost belligerent.

"Nothing serious, I assure you. Please don't worry; she'll live for years yet, most likely outlive you. Just don't let anything upset her; don't *you* upset her by fussing over her."

"Remember that, Papa," I said after the doctor left. "Don't let her see that you are concerned about her."

"Oh, Grace, she'll know. She could always tell what I had on my mind. Oh, very well, I'll do my best."

School reopened the following week, and as I got back onto a regular schedule we all settled down to a familiar routine. Carrie brought her "brood" over on

Sunday mornings to visit; Tom and Will, each with an infant daughter, usually came on Saturday afternoon, sometimes accompanied by their wives, but generally the Taylor girls were to be found at their parents' house across the street. We never knew when to expect Alfred. Sometimes a week would go by without our seeing him—or Ann or the boys—and then he would drop in two or three evenings in a row. On one of these occasions he told me privately that Ned Cochrane was a brick, but he didn't volunteer any information concerning his financial position. He couldn't seem to keep his mind on what was being said, and when Mamma asked me if I didn't think Alfred was looking poorly I was hard put to answer.

Fortunately my parents had plenty of friends who visited regularly: Mrs. Fitzy, as we called Mrs. Fitzgerald, would arrive in her elegant Packard; old Mr. and Mrs. Mayhew, who always came by taxi; and Mr. Frank Gallagher, an elderly bachelor (suspected to have been an old beau of Mamma's); and various other long-standing acquaintances, all of whom preferred to call at teatime rather than in the evening. It was rare, indeed, that I found my mother and father alone in the front parlor when I came in from school, and when this did occur they seemed at a loss and more or less expected me to entertain them with chitchat about the classroom or the teachers' lounge.

Ned, as I mentioned earlier, would come on Sunday afternoons and at times he stayed on for our light supper. At least it was supposed to be light, but Cook had her own ideas about what constituted a proper meal. Between tea and supper on one of those Sundays I went for a walk in the park with Ned, and it was then that he told me that he had arranged to lend my brother enough money to tide him over, and that he had also helped him construct a working budget. He warned me, though, that he could do nothing about keeping Alfred solvent unless Ann's extravagances were controlled. I thanked him for his generosity and told him that Alfred had said nothing further to me about his affairs, so that all I could do was to hope for the best. Later that evening, watching Alfred talking to Papa and Mamma, I tried to tell myself that he was looking better, but my mind was not easy about him.

October slipped away, a lovely month, with crisp, sunny days and cool nights, good nights for sleeping, as Papa said almost every morning. I wasn't actually unhappy, but neither was I satisfied with my life. I was teaching eighth grade and enjoying it, but what I really wanted to do was to hurry up and get my master's and teach at the college level. I thought of registering for some evening courses at NYU, but I was too late for the fall semester—and Papa would make such a fuss. He didn't fuss, though, when I began to go out to dinner and the theater with Ned; in fact, he was so effusive every time Ned called for me that I was embarrassed. Mamma was far more circumspect in her behavior. I wondered if she was remembering how her father acted when Frank Gallagher and Papa were courting her—maybe.

I can now see the reason, or, rather, the reasons for my underlying discontent. There were three: Ben, Rose, and Alfred. All my life I have hated open-endedness, inconclusion, and there seemed to be no end or conclusion to matters concerning those three. As I said earlier, I could put Rose and Ben in the back of my mind most of the time, but when it came to Alfred I simply worried.

And apparently I had reason to worry: early in November I arrived home from school one afternoon to find Mamma in tears, her lace-edged handkerchief pressed to her lips, Papa standing in front of the fire-place looking angry, and Alfred and Ann sitting as far apart from each other as the room would allow. There was silence as I stood in the doorway, and then Papa spoke in a voice that trembled with rage.

"Come in, Grace. You will have to know about this."

I cannot, I know, reproduce his faltering speech, so I'll give the facts in my own words:

1. Alfred was once again (so soon!) heavily in debt.
2. He had been asked to resign from his firm for "ungentlemanly behavior" (drinking).
3. They were being evicted from their house for nonpayment of rent.
4. There was nothing to do but take them in, bag and baggage.
5. They were to have the entire fourth floor, the rooms that Carrie, Tom, Will, and Alfred himself had had in the past. They would move in the next day.

My father enumerated the above points in an expressionless voice and left the room. Mamma made an effort to pull herself together, and after staring at the fire for a moment she turned to us.

"Yes, move in tomorrow, Alfred and Ann. We'll be ready for you."

Ann's "Thank you" was barely audible. Alfred did not speak, and they left quickly.

5

The most surprising thing about the next few weeks
was the change in Ann. She must have been humil-
iated and crestfallen by Alfred's disgrace, but I never
heard a word of complaint from her as she made the
necessary adjustments to a new and different way of
living. She established the boys in the front bedroom,
where they used Tom's and Will's old furniture, the
scarred and scratched schoolroom-type desks, the narrow iron beds, and the rickety bookshelf. She and Alfred took the larger, back bedroom directly above
mine, and little by little she fixed up the hall bedroom
as a tiny sitting room or study.

She took Charles and Francis out of their expensive
private school and sent them up to Sixty-eighth Street,
where I was teaching. I used to see them in the halls
from time to time, going about their business, two
quiet, well-behaved youngsters, who, I heard in the
teachers' lounge, were model pupils.

Then Ann went to work.

"I have a plan, Grace," she said one evening after

they had been with us for about three weeks. "And I'd like to know what you think of it."

We were in my room at the time. I had been correcting papers at my desk when she knocked on the door, a job I really wanted to finish, but when I turned and saw the anxious expression on her face I jumped up, pulled two chairs closer to the gas logs and invited her to sit down.

"I'm sure you know," she began, "how wretched this whole affair is for Alfred." It surprised me that she said "for Alfred," not "for me."

"He's absolutely miserable, ashamed, and frustrated. He isn't sleeping well, and you can see for yourself at meals that he eats very little; and he hardly talks at all."

I had noticed that, while I could hear them moving about in the room above, I almost never heard their voices.

"I was wondering if my plan would make things better or worse," she went on. "I thought that if I took a job—I could do that now that Charles and Francis are older—it would help us get back on our feet. But then I wondered if it might embarrass Alfred even more, having a working wife—"

"Ann, Alfred told me that you have an annuity—"

"Oh, Grace, I've turned over those payments to Ned Cochrane; they're only about a thousand a month, but they help a little in clearing those debts. I don't give them to Alfred anymore—"

"Do you mean you used to give your money to Alfred?"

"Every penny, at least for a while," she said ruefully. "He lost some money in the market last spring; you must have heard how stocks plunged then. He was so gullible—someone gave him a tip on a 'sure thing,' and he foolishly took it. Anyway, he tried to recoup by gambling and went deeper and deeper into debt, and there were even some threatening letters telling him to pay up. Part of it was my fault, you see. I wanted to live near Fifth and I wanted to send the boys to St. Paul's. I thought we could manage it, and I still think so if Alfred had been careful. But now we have nothing, less than nothing. If I could earn a little it couldn't but help, could it?"

I was too astonished to answer immediately. Which one was I to believe, my brother or my sister-in-law? She sounded completely plausible, sure of her facts, unhappy, but calm, whereas Alfred had been beside himself, distraught, and yes, inebriated.

"Grace?"

"Ann, how could you afford all those gorgeous clothes if you were giving your money to Alfred?"

"Oh, I did charge some things; it's so hard for me to resist Milgrim's dresses and suits—and then my mother, you know, adores taking me shopping and outfitting me. My grandmother, too."

"Well, what kind of job did you have in mind?"

"As a matter of fact I just heard of something. Ellen Lewiston's brother has opened a bookstore on Fifty-ninth Street, and she said he was looking for someone who could help out with sales and with records and things. It's close by, and the hours are good, and I do have the right sort of clothes. I could get Charles and Francis off to school in the morning before I go, and I'd be home by five-thirty. They'd be alone for only a couple of hours."

"I think it might work," I said slowly. "Possibly Katie or Maggie could take them to the park for an hour or so on nice afternoons. Yes, why don't you give it a try? As for Alfred, well, I scarcely think he's in a position to object."

She thanked me and left. I heard her footsteps as she crossed the room above, but I could hear no voices.

By Thanksgiving we were a fairly cheerful household. With Ned's help, Alfred was able to secure a position in the legal department of one of New York's larger banks, thank goodness. I wonder whether he ever realized how fortunate he was. Jobs were scarce in the fall of 1920, and unemployment was high. If he was aware of his good luck he never mentioned it; in fact, he had little to say about his work at all. He was quiet, but he was looking better.

Ann, on the other hand, had plenty to say and entertained us at dinner with stories of bookstore customers. Papa particularly liked the one about the fussy old gentleman who refused to remove his gloves while he examined a book, making it virtually impossible to turn a page. And then there was the one about the stylishly dressed and bejeweled society matron who thought Mr. Trollope was still alive and wondered when he would write another novel. No one could have made more of an effort than Ann did at that time, and I began to wonder why on earth Rose and I had ever put her down as a snob. Either she had never been one, or had gotten over being one, or we had completely misjudged her. In any case, she was turning out to be a thoroughly nice person.

As I said, things were going well. I think that in spite of the reason for it Papa was rather more pleased than not at having a full house again. And he did help; on several occasions it was he rather than Katie or

Maggie who took Charles and Francis to the zoo in the afternoon, and on rainy days the three of them could be found playing Parcheesi or some other board game. He was full of plans for Christmas, too. I heard him one morning telling Mamma that he was going down to Bloomingdale's to look around in the toy department to get some ideas for presents for the "little fellers." Oh, yes, when things were running smoothly Papa was as jovial as Mr. Pickwick under the mistletoe at Dingley Dell, but when he was worried or upset he could outdo Scrooge in irascibility. Mamma was always the more even-tempered of the two; her health may have been frail, but there was nothing wrong with her mind and she ran her enlarged household easily and competently.

Of course, Cook was delighted to be able to "really cook" again, as she put it. I'm sure she felt her talents were being wasted when there were just the three of us, but with seven at the big dining room table she could show what she could do. And she was genuinely fond of children, especially boys. When Charles and Francis came in from school she expected them to head straight for her kitchen, where she would set plates of Irish oatmeal cookies and glasses of milk out for them on the old wooden table.

Charles comes to visit me frequently now—he was here in the apartment only last week—and whenever he comes I am careful to have sandwiches or chocolate leaves for him to have with his tea, although I do order oatmeal cookies once in a while for myself. I wouldn't want to remind him of the brownstone house unnecessarily. Francis lives in California, and I hear from him only at Christmas time when he sends me pictures of his children, those shiny school pictures that are taken every year.

But that's the present; I must get back to November 1920.

When Cook heard that Alfred's family were to dine with the Kittredges on Thanksgiving Day, she was so dismayed at the thought of serving a holiday meal to only three people that Mamma quickly invited Carrie and her family. Tom and Will were scheduled to have dinner across the street with the Taylors, so Cook had to be satisfied with preparations for nine, although fifteen or sixteen would have made it a "grand feast."

Ordinarily we had dinner at seven in the evening, but out of consideration for Carrie's young ones, who were used to an early supper, we sat down just as the clock on the mantel struck five. Mamma had kept the children in mind when ordering the table decorations: a Jack Horner pie in the shape of a turkey rested on a silver tray in the center of the table, surrounded by miniature figures of Pilgrims and Indians. In addition, there were party favors, small dolls for the little girls and tiny fire engines for the boys. Papa always made a great show of carving: white meat for this one, dark for that one, and the wishbone for whoever could guess the number he had in mind. Mamma, at her end of the table, watched him with an amused smile, admonishing him every once in a while not to delay so much or everything would be cold.

The mince pie had been served (there were ice cream "shapes" for the children), homemade mincemeat, laced with Irish whiskey, naturally, and the hard sauce was being passed when Maggie came in with word that there was a lady to see me up in the front hall. (I should explain here that the bell sounded only in the kitchen and could not be heard in the dining room.)

"Ask her to wait in the parlor, Maggie," my father said sharply. He hated an interruption to any meal, and especially a holiday dinner, which he tended to prolong.

"It's probably one of your school friends, Grace. We'll make her welcome when we go upstairs for coffee and brandy, but she'll not interfere with our dinner."

When we finally rose from the table I managed to take Maggie aside to ask her if she knew the lady.

"Sure, and I don't know if I know her or not, Miss Grace—that dark was the veil she had covering her face."

I think I knew then that Rose had come home.

6

I'm not sure what I thought the heavy veil might have been hiding; perhaps I was afraid of seeing scars or bruises, I don't know, but I certainly was not prepared for the dull, vacant look in the eyes, those blue, blue eyes, set wide apart in a still beautiful face.

"Grace—" The voice was Rose's, but it was as dead and expressionless as the eyes, and just as disturbing.

Fortunately Maggie had put her in the front parlor. I knew the rest of the family would go directly to the larger back room, which had been opened up for the holiday weekend, and I thought I would have a few moments alone with my sister before they saw her. I closed the door and led her over to the sofa, where she sat severely erect, looking vaguely across the room and saying nothing further.

"Rose, Rose, are you ill? Look at me!"

She turned her head toward me, shook it slightly, and quickly looked away again. I made her stand up so that I could help her take off her coat, a cheap cloth affair that had seen better days. The dress underneath was not much better, a light blue silk that may have once matched her eyes but that was now not only faded and worn but also spotted with what looked like food stains on the bodice. This on Rose, who had always been so dainty and particular about her appearance! I started to ask her if her feet were wet and cold, thinking to get her a pair of my velvet slippers, when Katie knocked on the door and poked her head into the room.

"Miss Grace, Mr. Millerton says to bring your guest—why Miss Rose, Miss Rose!" Her voice rose to a shriek, and of course the rest of the family came running.

The scene that followed defies description. Suffice it to say that Mamma did not have a heart attack, that Papa was at a loss for words for only a moment, and that the prodigal son in the parable did not have a warmer reception than my sister. No one questioned her that night; she might have been gone for four days instead of four years as far as curiosity about her absence went. My parents and Carrie were so bent on making her feel welcome that I don't think they noticed how little she spoke—although Carrie might have. Then Alfred and his family came in and added to the hubbub. I noticed that Dr. Pelham was frowning as he watched Rose, but he said nothing and I had no chance to speak to him privately.

The children, who were all too young to remember Aunt Rose, showed little interest in her and soon disappeared to play with their toys in the hall and on the stairs. That's all that is clear in my mind concerning that part of the evening, but I do remember that before long Mamma said Rose must be tired and took her upstairs. I guess she assumed she'd had a long trip.

I must admit that I was none too pleased, when

upon going upstairs myself I found Rose in my room, tucked into her old bed in my newest embroidered nightgown, one with inserts of alençon lace. It had occurred to me once or twice over the past four years to get rid of our old brass beds and buy myself a comfortable, larger one, but it's just as well I never got around to it. Sleeping in the same bed with Rose would not have been at all to my liking, and I'm sure that's where Mamma would have put her. Where else was there?

I can now see how much I cherished the luxury of a room of my own, which I had never had until Rose eloped; we were always put together, in the brownstone house, in East Quogue, and even on the few occasions when Papa took us to Atlantic City for a spring vacation. I hadn't known what privacy was like in my earlier years, and now, not unnaturally, I suppose, I was loath to relinquish it.

My mother tiptoed around the room, motioning to me to be quiet, turning the lamps low (how was I to read in bed?), and left after a final, loving look at the motionless figure in the bed next to mine. I felt like crying.

It was Rose, however, who cried. Sometime during the night I was awakened by the sound of whimpering, short, gasping noises and sharp little cries that reminded me of a kitten we once had who had been hurt by one of the homeless cats in the backyard. She didn't answer me when I spoke to her, and by the time I lighted a lamp and carried it over to look at her, the whimpering had stopped and she appeared to be sleeping quietly. Toward morning she awakened me a second time, and after that there was no getting back to sleep.

I lay there wondering what on earth I was to do. I've always needed a good eight hours' sleep in order to function well and I knew that if that Thanksgiving night were any indication of the nights to come, I would become cross, irritable, and, more important, unable to teach properly. I considered the possible solutions: could Rose be put in Ann's little sitting room? I didn't think Mamma would consent to that. Should I move out? I could afford a small apartment, and I was certainly old enough to be on my own. But Papa would have a fit. Should I marry Ned? And live with Mrs. Cochrane?

It was still very early, but I slipped out of bed, and taking the necessary clothing with me went into the bathroom to dress. My sister did not stir; Rose, thou art sick, I thought as I left the room, wondering just how sick she was and how long the illness would last.

"Grace, you look exhausted! Come in. Put those packages down. What are you doing out so early?" Dr. John Pelham looked concerned as he helped me take off my coat. Mamma had sent me out right after breakfast to buy some articles of clothing for Rose, and on my way home from Bloomingdale's I stopped in at Carrie's husband's office in Sixty-first Street.

"I think I know what's on your mind," he went on. "She looked pretty bad last night, and you're worried."

I didn't tell him that I was more upset by my bad night than I was worried about Rose; I merely asked him if he didn't think she needed medical attention.

"Of course she does, Grace. One look at her would tell you that. But we'll have to go slowly. She's obviously had a bad experience, and I wouldn't advise you to try to get her to tell you about it yet. That might do more harm than good at this point. How was she this morning?"

"When I left she was having breakfast in bed. She said very little, just yes, no, thank you. She cried during the night—" And I described the whimpering sounds.

"And you got very little sleep. If this goes on, and it may, it will wear you out, Grace. Isn't there another room someplace?"

"Only the hall bedroom, Alfred's old room. And Ann uses that as a sitting room. All we need now is to have Tom and Will move in with their families. . . . I've been thinking of taking an apartment for myself, but I'm afraid of being excommunicated. They'd say I was an ungrateful, unloving, unnatural sister, and maybe I am, John."

"Nonsense. You're a perfectly normal, hard-working schoolteacher who needs her sleep and her privacy. Look, I'll stop in late today on my way home. And in the meantime I'll have a word with Bronson. Perhaps we'll come up with something."

I hurried home to find Rose still in bed. My parents were sitting in their usual chairs in the front parlor looking considerably less exhuberant than on the previous evening. When I told them that Dr. John would stop in later Mamma nodded, and Papa said maybe he'd give Rose a tonic. I hadn't the heart to tell them I wanted her out of my room. I think I really wanted her out of my life.

The nights that followed were pretty much a repetition of the first one, and by the end of the week I was worn out. I hated the thought of going into my room and, worse than that, I had begun to hate Rose. She was docility itself, allowing the specialists Dr. John and Dr. Bronson brought in to examine her, and dutifully taking the medication they prescribed, but she refused to leave the room except to use the bathroom next to it.

At that point the doctors seemed to think that her nervous system had sustained a severe shock from which she might or might not recover. The whimpering at night, they said, might even be good for her, a release of some sort. Well, if that was the case, I thought bitterly, I needed to be released from such a release.

And so with Ann's help I converted the little sitting room back into a bedroom and moved up to the fourth floor. I was glad that the room was in the front of the house, next to the boys' room, and not directly beside Ann and Alfred in the rear. It was two or three days before Mamma realized that Rose now slept alone. She said nothing at first, but the look she gave me was the kind I imagine one would turn on a deserter or a traitor, and her attitude toward me became decidedly cool.

Although my new bedroom was small, dark, and overcrowded with even the few pieces of essential furniture, moving into it probably saved my sanity. And the move improved my relationship with my brother and his family. Charles and Francis, sometimes together but more often separately, would drop in during the evening to ask for help with assignments, to show me a paper with a gold star on it, or just to say goodnight. And Alfred came, too. He was beginning to seem more like his old self, fooling with the boys just before bedtime, and then coming in to sit with me for a few minutes. Ann was obviously enjoying her work at the bookstore—in fact, that branch of the family seemed to be on an even keel at last. Occasionally Alfred would go down to the kitchen late in the evening and bring up a tray of cake or cookies, and then the three of us would sit in their room and talk. Of course we talked about Rose . . .

I've been wondering lately whether Rose's trouble

made Alfred reassess his position and count his blessings; sometimes people have strange reactions to misfortune. Rose's return and her condition made me impatient and brought out a streak of selfishness in my character; it had the opposite effect on Alfred. Perhaps Francis Bacon was right about adversity not being without its comforts and hopes. Mamma, however, was finding little comfort in anything; she was changing before our eyes from a complacent, light-hearted woman into a grim-faced, taciturn old lady.

We all looked in on Rose at least once a day; even Charles and Francis paid short visits, and Alfred and Ann usually went in for a few minutes after dinner while the boys did their homework. It was hard to stay with Rose for any length of time, though, since all efforts at conversation died aborning, what with her monosyllabic, disinterested answers to questions. I would generally stop in to see her on my way upstairs after school before going down for tea. Some days she would be on the chaise longue idly stroking Pumpy, who liked the warmth of the afghan she had over her legs, and at other times I would find her standing at the window, with her head pressed against the glass.

"Rose, for pity's sake!" I burst out one afternoon when I found her staring out at the snow that had started earlier and was now falling steadily. "Why don't you make an effort? You could get well! Whatever happened to you is over and done with—"

I was so exasperated with her that day that I took hold of her shoulders—I think I was about to shake her—but she looked at me with such terror (the first real expression of any kind I had seen since her return) that I let her go.

"Rosie, can't you tell me? You used to tell me everything. How did you get here? Where did you come from? Where is Jack Egerton? Tell me, Rose. Remember how we used to lie in bed at night and talk and talk and talk?"

"Your bed is no longer close enough for her to confide in you at night, Grace," Mamma said coldly as she came into the room carrying her knitting bag. "Go down and have your tea. Papa is alone in the parlor."

She's really turned on me, I thought, as I went downstairs to my father, feeling like a disobedient child.

"No zoo today, Papa?" I asked as I poured my tea. He put his paper aside and held out his cup for me to refill.

"No, Grace," he answered rather crossly. "No zoo. Katie has the boys. They took their sleds to the park; won't stay long in this cold, I should think. No, no, I didn't want to go out, and I didn't want to leave your mother alone. Couldn't expect anyone to call in this weather. And now she's left me alone—gone up to your sister. And she's changed, my dear—your mother, I mean. She's not herself at all. This business of Rose—I thought things would go back to being the way they were before, before she ran off, you know. And all the doctors will say is give her time, give her time. But how much time? How much time do your mother and I have left? Good God, what's that noise?"

"It's just the boys, Papa, bumping their sleds down the areaway steps," I said, looking out the front window. "It's only two days until Christmas, you know, and they're terribly excited."

I watched Katie start down the steps after them— poor soul, she looked half frozen—and then I saw someone right behind her at the entrance to the areaway. Whoever it was paused for a moment before going on; probably just a pedestrian catching his

70

breath before hurrying home through the storm, I thought, but it did seem odd that he'd been following Katie and the boys so closely.

"I'm jumpy as a cat these days," Papa was saying as I turned away from the window. "I guess this is all getting to me, too. Be a good girl, Grace, and see if the children want to play a game with an old man. Might take my mind off things."

To take my own mind off things I went upstairs to wrap Christmas presents afer I saw the Parcheesi game under way. Red ribbon and white tissue paper, the only wrappings we ever used in those days, were spread out on my desk, and I was taking boxes down from the closet shelf when I thought I heard footsteps on the stairs.

"Is that you, Ann? Come and see what I found for Charles!"

There was no answer, and then I realized it was not yet five o'clock, too early for either Ann or Alfred to be home. I put the packages down and went out into the hall, where the gas jet was burning low, as usual. I turned it up, but could see no one on the stairs. The other two bedrooms on the fourth floor were in darkness.

I ran down to the floor below, and as I reached the bottom of the stairs Rose came out of the bathroom, closed the door, and without turning her head in my direction went quickly and silently into her own room. As I have already mentioned, the bathroom on that floor had three doors, one opening into each bedroom and one into the hall. It was a long, narrow room, with two old-fashioned marble sinks, one at each end, and a large tub encased in wood in the middle. The toilet, standing on a marble pedestal, was separated from the tub and sinks by somewhat flimsy wooden partitions.

One of the three gas jets was always kept lit, but even when all three were on, parts of the bathroom remained in semidarkness. I wasn't ever tempted to take the long leisurely baths (there was never enough hot water anyway) there that I do now in my warm, cheerful bathroom with its flowered wallpaper above the gleaming tile. I was always afraid I had forgotten to lock one of the doors, or that I would forget to unlock one of them when I left. Nothing made Papa crosser than to find the door leading to his bedroom locked on the bathroom side, especially if he had to get up during the night.

I wondered briefly why Rose had not gone directly from the bathroom into her room, as she usually did, instead of using the hall door, but I knew that in her present uncommunicative state it would be useless to ask her. I went slowly back upstairs to my Christmas wrapping, but not without a nagging thought that I was letting something go, that there was something I should look into.

And I didn't feel any better when Alfred said at dinner that he had found the outside areaway door half open when he came home.

"I came in that way tonight because I was covered with snow from head to foot. And you boys left your sleds where anyone might fall over them. After dinner go and stand them up where they belong." And he smiled at them to show that the offense was not too serious.

"I guess we forgot because we were holding the door for Katie; she was so cold," Charles said. "And then Aunt Grace called us to play Parcheesi with Grandpa."

"All right, all right, all is forgiven. Just stand them up properly as soon as you've finished."

Then I knew what had been bothering me: I hadn't heard the iron door clang shut.

"Grace, did you hear someone moving around last night? I thought maybe Francis was walking in his sleep. He used to do that once in a while when he was younger, but when I looked they were both in bed."

Ann frowned, and when she pushed her hair back from her face I thought she looked paler than usual.

"Oh, I must have imagined it," she went on after I had denied hearing anything. "Alfred says I have enough imagination to persuade myself the Seventh Regiment is coming up the stairs. Look, I must run; this will be a busy, busy day with all the last-minute shoppers. Thank heaven we're closing early; I'll be home by four, I hope. It's so good of you, Grace, to take the boys." And she was off.

It was Christmas Eve, a cold, gray day with the threat of more snow, a day to sit by the fire and read, or to find an excuse to spend some time in the savory warmth of the kitchen, where Cook would be in her element. Oddly enough, the more complicated the culinary preparations, the more she delighted in having an audience; professional pride, I suppose. But I had promised to take Charles and Francis down Fifth Avenue to see the window displays, to visit at least one toy department, and to help them finish their Christmas shopping.

I was on my way upstairs to get my purse when Mamma called to me from her room.

"Grace, one moment, please—"

She didn't look at all well; her face was drawn, her eyes tired, and her hands were unsteady as she put her sewing down on the table next to her chair. She smiled as she looked at me, not her old joyous smile, but a small, sad one.

"I want to say this, Grace, just once, and you must believe me: old people sometimes turn against others for a very poor reason, or for no reason at all, and sometimes they turn against the very ones they love the most."

She didn't have to go on; she was a woman of few words, and this was, I knew, as much of an apology or explanation of her conduct as she thought necessary. Nor did she expect me to say anything in reply, so I kissed her cold cheek lightly, and after telling her where I was going I set off with my nephews.

"Aunt Grace, may we sit on top of the bus?"

"Aunt Grace, maybe we ought to see Santa Claus after all—we don't believe in him anymore, but just the same—"

"Will we have lunch in Schrafft's? I'm hungry already."

I said yes to everything; they were such reasonable, appreciative children that one was inclined to accede to their requests without hesitating. Reasonable! That word comes to mind every time I think of that Christmas. Everyone in the household tried so hard to *be* reasonable, to strike the right note, the note that would help make it a good Christmas without forced cheer. Genuine merriment was out of the question; it had been since Thanksgiving.

The outing, if somewhat tiring, was completely successful: we got off the bus at Fortieth Street and walked down the west side of the avenue, stopping to admire the windows in Lord and Taylor's, Franklin Simon's, and Best's. On Thirty-fourth Street, we went into a small curio shop that specialized in inexpensive but colorful articles from the East. Francis bought a small temple bell for Ann, and when I asked him what she would use it for he answered that perhaps she could ring it when she wanted him to get up in the morning. Charles was enchanted with a little curved paper-knife, or letter opener, shaped like a small scimitar. The handle and the case into which the blade fitted were of polished bamboo, embellished with what looked like a Persian rug design to me.

"I'll get it for Aunt Rose," he said happily. "She can open all her letters with it."

I forbore telling him that Rose hadn't received a single letter since her return, but I did warn him against playing with it himself; it was wickedly sharp. When he promised to leave the blade in its sheath I let him buy it.

From there we went over to Altman's—their windows were marvelous—where the two of them took what seemed to me an interminable length of time picking out modest presents for their father. That accomplished, they were more than ready for lunch at the nearest Schrafft's, after which we headed back to Altman's and up to the toy floor, Santa and all. It was snowing as we started for home, and the uptown bus was so slow that I bundled the boys off it and into a taxi at Forty-second Street. Even so, we were late getting back to Sixty-fifth Street; the tea things had been cleared away and there was just time to brush up for the evening meal.

Christmas Eve "supper," as Cook called it, always consisted of a huge tureen of fish stew, a mixture of lobster, crab, shrimp, and I don't know what else simmered in a wonderful sherry-flavored sauce. This was accompanied by thick slices of her homemade bread, followed by fruit for dessert. We used to say that the 24th of December was the only day of the year Cook showed any restraint in what she sent in to the dining room because she wanted us all to be ravenous for the next day's feast. We were probably right.

Later in the evening, as we were putting the finishing touches on the big tree in the back parlor, Ned came over with my present.

"Mother said you probably read this in serial form last summer in the *Pictorial Review*, Grace, but I was pretty sure you were too busy with Shakespeare and Milton then," he said as he handed me Mrs. Wharton's new novel.

The Age of Innocence, with "Grace, from Ned, Christmas, 1920" written on the flyleaf, is still in my possession. I reread sections of it from time to time, perhaps because I see a strong resemblance between our own brownstone-controlled lives and the society-ruled existence of the Wellands and the Archers. And the furnishings Mrs. Wharton describes! Our back parlor could have come straight out of one of her Old New York tales.

We were all gathered in the green velvet splendor of that room, my parents sitting in the large armchairs close to the fireplace, while Alfred, Ann, and the children crowded onto the sofa and Ned and I sat on the loveseat a little apart from the others. We had been singing Christmas carols, and in the moment of silence that followed the last notes of "Adeste Fideles" we heard a door slam some place upstairs.

"Grace, will you see if Rose—" Mamma began.

"I'll go, Mrs. Millerton," Ann said quickly. "It's time I took these two up anyway. Come on, boys, your stockings have been hung, and now there's nothing for you but a long winter's nap."

Ned did not stay long after that; his mother was expecting him for a late supper.

"How about a snowy walk in the park tomorrow afternoon, Grace?" he asked as I saw him to the door. "You'll probably be ready for some fresh air after the Christmas morning excitement."

I said I'd love it, and then ran upstairs to check on Rose. She was already in bed and, from what I could see by the light of the lowered gas flame, asleep. I closed her door gently and went on up to the fourth floor to collect my presents in order to put them under the tree. Ann was standing at my end of the hall, just outside the door to the boys' room, clutching the newel post of the stairs leading to the maids' floor and looking up. When she saw me she started and then motioned to me to follow her into her room. She looked so ashen that I thought she was going to faint, and when I guided her over to one of the easy chairs I felt a tremor run through her body. It took her a moment to get control of herself, and when she spoke her voice was hoarse with fright.

"There's someone, Grace, there's someone in this house! I heard footsteps, I heard them!"

"Ann, Ann, don't tell me you're imagining the Seventh Regiment again!" Alfred came quickly across the room, pulled her up out of the chair, and held her close to him.

"Darling, Ann darling, you've got to get over this. Look, it's an old, old house; it creaks with age, but it's just a house. It can't hurt you."

"But it can frighten me. I'm scared to death!"

"Ann, when you came up with the boys was Rose in bed?"

"Yes, I think she was asleep. I don't know who could have slammed that door—"

"It probably was a door in the kitchen," Alfred said comfortably, still cradling Ann in his arms. "With all these stairs and hallways you can't always tell from which direction a sound comes. I know we all thought it was an upstairs door, but we could all be wrong. Look, you two, I'll go down and find some cake or something. We didn't have a real dessert."

I had noticed recently that Alfred couldn't seem to get enough sweets and wondered if it had anything to do with his giving up drinking. (I have since read that this is quite often the case.)

After he left, Ann looked at me questioningly. I nodded; I didn't have to say anything. We had both heard unidentified footsteps, no matter what Alfred thought. We sat quietly, listening, until he came back with a tray of cookies and milk. He wouldn't let us talk about footsteps or doors slamming, so I didn't stay long. As soon as I could I went back to my own room, where I sat down at the desk and wrote something like this:

1. On the 23rd, I thought I heard footsteps on the stairs between the third and fourth floors, about 4:45 P.M.

2. At dinner that night Alfred said he had

found the outside areaway door partly
open.

3. That same night Ann thought she
heard someone moving about on the
fourth floor.

4. On the 24th, when we were all in the
back parlor (except Rose), we heard a
door slam. Was Rose really asleep?

5. A short time later Ann heard footsteps
on the stairs to the fifth floor.

6. Why does Alfred persist in taking this
all so lightly?

I was so upset when I finished writing that I nearly
forgot to put my presents under the tree in the back
parlor.

C H A P T E R

8

Ned was right; by three o'clock on Christmas afternoon I was more than ready to escape from the excitement and confusion of our household. The morning hadn't been too bad, but shortly after lunch, which was early that day (and very light), we had an almost steady stream of visitors, most of them bearing gifts. The entire parlor floor, including the front hall and the little-used music room, was littered with crumpled tissue paper, empty boxes, and discarded ribbon. Children, notably Carrie's, ran around unheeded, helping themselves liberally to the Christmas candy Papa had provided.

"All those sticky little fingers," I heard Maggie mutter as she picked up some of the wrappings. "Think of the marks on the tables and the madam's best chairs!"

But Mamma did not seem to notice; her mind was half on Rose, I guess. My poor sister—when I looked in on her just before lunch she was lying on the chaise longue with the afghan over her feet and the pile of our presents still unopened beside her. The canary

Mamma had commissioned me to buy ("It will be company for her, Grace") chirped unheeded in its cage in the sunny window.

Rose opened her eyes as I approached, but closed them immediately. I knew it was useless to try to interest her in the packages or to try to light a spark of life in that immobile face. Even anger would have been better than the blankness I saw, so I just stood looking down at her, feeling helpless. She was dressed that morning (sometimes she didn't bother and spent the whole day in a robe or negligee) in a soft blue silk, which made her look the very picture of youth and innocence. Whatever experience she had undergone during her absence had left no mark or line on her flawless complexion—just emptiness.

A knock on the door roused me, and Katie sailed in with a tray.

"Miss Rose, dear, here's yer lunch. And Cook will be that put out if you don't eat all of it. Now be a good girl, come." And she set the food on a table near the fireplace.

To my surprise, Rose smiled, got up quickly, agilely, and settled herself comfortably in front of the table. While her back was turned I pretended to arrange her presents and managed to slip Charles' little box into my skirt pocket. I knew I should have had more sense than to have let him buy such a dangerous instrument; in Rose's state, I thought, she might easily turn it on herself, and I had enough to worry about without that.

"Katie, you're wonderful with her," I said as we went down together. "Really you are. Maybe if you tried you could get her to talk to you. Would you have time to spend a few minutes with her?"

"It's only at meals, Miss Grace, that she comes to life. She's that hungry these last days. And she never gains a bit; built like a child, she is. Cook says she needs fattening up and rejoices every time the tray comes back looking as if Jack Sprat and his wife had been at it."

It must be part of her illness, I thought. Rose had never, in the old days, been a hearty eater. Then I remembered reading that people sometimes ate out of boredom, and, goodness knows, Rose's life must certainly have been filled with long, boring days.

As I said, our own lunch was a light one, so that when Ned bought a bag of peanuts for us to throw to the squirrels I ate most of them. He laughed when I told him how Cook had been half starving us since the previous day so that we would do justice to her Christmas banquet, and said he wished he could join us.

"You know you'd be welcome, Ned."

"Yes, I know, and I'd love it, but Mother has asked some people and she's counting on me to play host. She wanted to invite you, too, but I knew you'd be expected at home. I wish you were coming, though."

The park was lovely that afternoon. The sun was bright, the snow underfoot was crunchy, and the air was filled with the shouts of children as they tried out their new Christmas sleds.

"Flexible Flyers, every one, I warrant," Ned murmured as we watched a group of little boys coast down one of the slopes.

We strolled as far north as the obelisk, and then, as the sun was lower in the sky, we turned and walked back more briskly. I stumbled slightly on an uneven patch of snow, and when Ned caught me he pulled my arm through his and held it firmly, close to his side.

"One thing we don't need is a twisted ankle," he said smiling down at me, his lean, handsome face close to mine. His dark eyes were so full of concern,

82

admiration, love—I don't know what—that my heart skipped a beat, and I felt myself blushing.

"You're smiling, Grace. Tell me—"

"I really don't know why I'm smiling, Ned," I said quickly. "With all the trouble in the house I've no right to. I guess it's just a relief to be out for a while."

He thought I meant Rose, and somehow I couldn't tell him about the other thing, the footsteps and all.

"What's needed, Grace, is a companion for Rose. Or an institution. It isn't right for the whole family to dance attendance on her. The strength of the weak, you know, can be too much for the strong."

He was right, of course, but I knew my parents would never consider either alternative. I wouldn't even make the suggestion to them.

As we crossed Fifth Avenue on the way home, I saw a chauffeured limousine draw up in front of the Astor house; a woman swathed in furs, sable, I imagine, emerged from the car and walked quickly across the carefully cleared pavement to the wide front entrance. Lights shone in almost all the windows, and when we looked down over the iron railing around the moat we could see uniformed maids and menservants moving about in bustling activity behind the large, barred windows. It all looked so safe in there; I envied the occupants, who would surely be insulated against footsteps in the night and who would have nurses around the clock for an invalid.

We were back at our front stoop when Ned took a small package from his coat pocket and handed it to me.

"This is your real present, Grace dear. I hope you will wear it." And he walked quickly away.

I knew it would be a piece of jewelry; the box was that size. What would I do if it contained a ring?

Maybe I'd wear it; that would mean we were engaged; that would mean marriage; that would mean living in the Cochrane house.

But when I opened the box in the privacy of my room I was delighted (or was I disappointed?) to see a lavaliere set with amethysts of various shades of purple and lavender, suspended from a delicate gold chain. I wore it that night at dinner, but Ann was the only one who noticed it.

"It's lovely, Grace," she said softly as we sat in the back parlor sipping coffee. "Tiffany's?" She must have known Ned had given it to me, for she didn't ask.

"Yes," I replied. "And yours?" She was wearing a pin I had not seen before, a circle of diamonds that looked worth a king's ransom.

"I don't know where this came from; it's been in the family for generations, an heirloom, I guess. My mother didn't want it any more. Father bought her a larger one, so it came to me. I could take it to Tiffany's and see. I understand they always have an identifying mark on their jewelry. I'd be interested to know what it's worth too. Maybe I'll run down there tomorrow on my lunch hour."

"Tomorrow and tomorrow—what about tomorrow except that it's back to the workaday world?" Alfred brought his cup over to where we were sitting.

"Not for me. Teachers are off until after New Year's."

"And children, too," Ann said. "Did I tell you, Grace, that the boys are going to Lake Placid with my parents for a week? They're annoyed at me for not going, but I don't like to ask Bob Lewiston for time off just now."

I had planned to take Charles and Francis to a couple of matinees, as well as to the Museum of Natural

84

History, and felt slightly disappointed. Then, on the other hand, I knew I would be glad to have time to myself, to refurbish my wardrobe, to see some friends for lunch, or just to do nothing. But I didn't like the idea of an empty room next to mine. What on earth is coming over me, I wondered. The presence of two youngsters next door to me was comforting, but certainly no protection. And protection against what? Footsteps? I shuddered and had to pretend to feel a draught when Alfred asked me what was wrong.

We were a subdued family group that night, sitting over our coffee. The big room reflected this mood—or maybe it created it: order had been restored, by Maggie probably, and with the exception of the Christmas tree, which would not be dismantled until the day after New Year's, the room was ready to be closed up again until Easter. What a waste, I thought, picturing my own cramped quarters up on the fourth floor.

"Come over near the fire, Grace," Papa said, pulling up a chair for me next to Mamma. "We're not a very lively family tonight, are we? Why is it always like this on Christmas night, as if a balloon had been pricked?" Poor Papa, he hated a party to end.

"I think we're all tired, James," my mother said. "So much going on, and all . . ." Her voice trailed off.

"Well, I can't wait to get my heels into bed," Ann said as she started for the door. The rest of us followed almost at once, and if there were any footsteps that night they went unheard.

9

"Your mother is having her breakfast with your sister, Grace. She said she was too tired to face the stairs this morning. Do you think we should ask Bronson to have another look at her?" My father looked anxiously at me as he spoke.

"She slept all night," he went on. "I'm quite certain of that. I fail to see why she isn't rested. What are we going to do, how will we manage, if she takes to staying up there? She spends half her time with Rose as it is, and I don't like it. I don't like it at all."

"Perhaps we ought to see about having a nurse, or a companion of some sort, to come in and take care of Rose," I ventured. "That would relieve Mamma."

"Nonsense, absolute nonsense! Why does a perfectly healthy young woman need someone to be with her day and night? And I won't have strangers in the house, do you hear? Call Bronson, will you? I want to talk to him, get a few things straight." And he stormed out of the dining room without finishing his coffee.

Things were not going his way at all. He wanted my

mother at breakfast with him, and sitting in the front parlor where he could see her, and he wanted Rose to be the Rose of four years ago. He didn't want change, and he didn't want to have to worry about Mamma. He was, when one comes right down to it, a completely self-centered man.

He didn't feel any better after Dr. Bronson's visit. When he heard that Rose's recovery would take time and patience, and that Mamma should avoid exertion as much as possible, with stairs only once a day and plenty of rest, he didn't say anything, but his mood did not improve. I should mention that he rarely spent any time with Rose; he found her unnatural appearance unnerving, I think. On one occasion when I saw him trying to talk to her I thought he looked embarrassed, as if he had been caught doing something improper. Enough of my father; I must get on.

I wanted to talk to the doctor privately, so after lunch I stopped in at his office. He saw me at once; I think he was glad to be able to talk freely about our situation without fear of an emotional outbreak.

"First of all, your mother's heart is weakening, giving out as a muscle, and unable to function as a good pump for the circulation. She could live for a good while yet, but then again, she might go at any time. See that she takes her medication and keep her calm—that's about all one can do.

"Then there's Rose: we're pretty sure now that she has a form of schizophrenia. The flat, monotonous voice, the expressionless face, the lack of response to people and events, all symptoms of the disease, are present in Rose. Unfortunately, we don't know a great deal about it yet; the disease didn't even have a name until ten years ago, and its cause is uncertain, its cure unknown. But we do know that it has phases: Rose

may come out of this apathy and be bright and cheerful, her old self, for a while, and then lapse back into a
withdrawn state again. Or she may pull out of it completely. It's been known to happen. That's about all I
can tell you, Grace. I know it's not reassuring, but you
should know the truth of the matter."

I felt rather depressed myself as I left his office and
tried to distract my mind by exchanging Christmas
presents. Carrie had given Mamma gloves that were
too small, Papa wanted a blue scarf instead of a red
one, and even Katie asked me to exchange some lavender water for lily of the valley.

"Lavender belongs to your mother, Miss Grace," she
said. "It wouldn't feel right on me."

Bloomingdale's was full of people doing exactly
what I was doing—only to be expected on December
26th—and the clerks were so busy that it was almost
four when I left the store. I was in no hurry to get back
to the gloom of our house, so I walked west on Fifty-
ninth Street over to Fifth Avenue. The sun was low in
the sky, ready to sink behind the houses down beyond
Columbus Circle, but still casting a soft glow on the
snowy park. I was not the only one who chose to daw-
dle that day; I noticed other strollers who, with the
rush of Christmas preparations behind them, seemed
to have slowed down, taken time, as it were, to catch
their breath and savor the peace of a windless winter
afternoon. I wondered how many New Yorkers knew
what a debt of gratitude they owed to Frederick Law
Olmsted . . .

I was glad to see Mamma having tea with Papa in
the front parlor when I got home. She poured me a
cup, and after the exchanges were approved told me
that the doctor had recommended that she put her feet
up on a footstool whenever she could.

"I think there's one in the storeroom on the top floor, Grace. I seem to remember putting it up there years ago; it was always getting in the way, and people tripped over it."

"Damn near broke my neck on it once. But if the doctor says you need it, my dear—"

"Grace, when you're rested a bit, would you go up and see if it's there? Here's the key to the storeroom. Be sure you lock the door when you come out. Oh, and Grace, take a flashlight with you; there's no gas fixture in there."

The last thing I wanted to do was to go up through the empty house to the fifth floor alone. I should have gone down to the kitchen and asked Katie or Maggie to go with me, but Mamma, from where she sat in the parlor, had a clear view of the stairs and would have seen us and asked questions, so I had to go by myself. I procrastinated a bit; I spent a few minutes with Rose, I tidied my hair, I washed my hands, and when I could think of nothing else to do I turned up the gas light in the fourth floor hall as high as it would go and started up the stairs. I got to the halfway point when I remembered the flashlight. I did not have one of my own, but I knew that Charles did, because Ann caught him reading in bed with it one night. It took me a few more minutes to find it among the jumble of small-boy treasures in his desk, and when I tested it I could see that the batteries were too weak to be of much use.

This time I ran up the whole flight of stairs—to get it over with—and had to stand at the top to catch my breath. The three bedroom doors were closed, and the one to the bathroom only partly open. That bathroom had a skylight, which could be opened for ventilation, and when I pushed the door back as far as it would go, I could see that this was a far more cheerful room than its counterparts on the floors below. But I couldn't stop to examine it closely; for one thing I hadn't time, and for another I felt uncomfortable, as if I were on someone else's property. I fitted the key into the lock of the door alongside the bathroom, and although it turned smoothly I could not push the door open. I rattled the knob, turned the key again, leaned against the heavy door as hard as I could, and then removed the key and bent over to see if, with the aid of the flashlight, I could find any obstruction in the keyhole. As I straightened up, at least I think that's how it was, and before I fainted, I felt a hand on my shoulder.

10

When I came to, Katie was bending over me holding the bottle of lily of the valley cologne under my nose.

"Mother of God, Miss Grace, what is it yer after doing? The Mister sent me up to see what was keeping you so long, and there you were all in a heap. Are ye hurt any?"

Then it couldn't have been Katie's hand. I can still remember how it felt: it wasn't just someone touching my shoulder to make me aware of his presence; it was the strong grip of a person who was angry or frightened, or both. Someone with large hands.

I told Katie I had run up the stairs too fast and swore her to secrecy about my fainting. Then I went down to the parlor and reported that the door was impossible to open.

"Not surprising, not at all surprising," Papa said. "No one's looked in there for years. Probably everything in the storeroom is rotted away. Look, my dear, tomorrow I'll get you the best footstool that can be had. I'll go down to Sloane's first thing. Always did like that store."

"But James, Alfred can probably open the door when he comes in. It must be stuck, and a good hard push—" Mamma began.

"But I want you to have a new one, not some old dusty thing."

"What difference does it make? It's just to put my feet on—oh, all right, do as you please. You will anyway."

She knew it was useless to try to talk him out of his shopping trip; he'd buy a new footstool now even if the old one did turn up.

I must have been listening to them because I remember the conversation clearly, but my mind was on the coming night. Alfred and Ann, taking advantage of the boys' absence, were dining with friends and going on to the theater afterward. They'd be late. And I'd be alone on the fourth floor for hours.

I couldn't tell my parents what had happened, I simply couldn't. Dr. Bronson had not been at all sanguine about Mamma's condition and he'd emphasized the importance of keeping her from worrying. But it wasn't just on her account that I didn't dare call the police; Papa, like others of his generation and social position, held that summoning help from the law was somehow or other a disgrace, an invasion of privacy, a sign that the master of the house could not manage his own affairs. I've already mentioned his reaction to my suggestion that we get a nurse for Rose, so you can imagine his wrath at the thought of policemen searching his house for a person no one had even seen.

I thought of calling Ned for advice, but the only telephone in the house was on the wall in the front hall, just outside the front parlor, which made holding a private conversation almost impossible. In any case, I was to lunch with him at the Plaza Hotel the next day, and I could tell him then, if I could just get through the night.

My parents went to bed shortly after nine o'clock, and a little while later I saw Cook and the maids slip quietly up the stairs. It was my intention to stay in the parlor reading *The Age of Innocence* until Alfred and Ann came in and go up with them. I could say I waited up to hear about the play they saw. I didn't think I would tell them what had happened; Ann would believe me, but my brother would scoff and chalk it up to an overactive imagination, or else say it must have been Katie's hand. But maybe it would be wiser, I thought, not to tell Ann; she was upset enough as it was.

After an eternity, the clock on the mantel struck ten. I gave up all pretence of reading (even Mrs. Wharton couldn't hold my attention that night) and sat staring at the dying fire, wondering how much longer I could make myself stay there.

Out of the corner of my eye I saw one of the portieres move slightly, which should not have disturbed me, because in that draughty old house they often swayed a little, especially when the damper in the fireplace was open. But things were not normal that night, not even the familiar inanimate objects within my field of vision. The room was too quiet, the ticking of the clock too loud, the shadow cast by Mamma's workbasket on the carpet was in the shape of a grotesque, elongated skull. I couldn't seem to move any part of me except my eyes. The room became colder, and as it did I felt closer and closer to panic. I was in an impossible situation, afraid to go upstairs, afraid to stay where I was, and afraid I was going out of my wits.

The sound of a log settling between the andirons decided me; I jumped so when I heard it that before I knew what I was doing I was halfway up the stairs. I burst into Rose's room with a wild idea of getting, fully dressed, into my old bed, but the sight of her lying there sound asleep brought me to my senses, and making as little noise as possible I fled up the next flight of stairs, down the dimly lit hall and into my small bedroom, where I jammed the desk chair against the door. Hours later, after my heart had stopped pounding, and after I heard Alfred and Ann come in, I managed to sleep.

I was late going down to breakfast the next day. Ann finished her coffee as I took my place at the table and hurried off, saying she had to be at the bookstore early since she was responsible for the inventory they were in the process of taking.

"That girl will go far," Papa said approvingly. "She'd be an asset to any store. And she takes the work seriously. Wouldn't surprise me if she ended up owning the place."

He was dressed up that morning, wearing what he called his "company" suit, in honor of the trip down to Sloane's, and he seemed pleased with the world that day. Mamma was there to pour his coffee, the bacon was crisp, the sun was shining, and he was going off to buy a footstool. When I said that I would be lunching with Ned he fairly beamed.

"Yes, Ann is a dear," Mamma said as she handed me the marmalade. "She's bringing up her children to be so well mannered and she's so sweet with Rose."

At the mention of my sister's name Papa's face clouded over, but before he could say anything Alfred asked him what he thought president-elect Harding's position on taxes would be, which served to distract him. Whether Alfred purposely diverted my father's attention or not I cannot say, but I rather think he did. Over the years we had all learned to watch for the warning signals and had become adept at heading off grumpiness or displeasure. It was even more important to keep Papa in a good mood than to please Cook.

He left with Alfred, saying that since it was such a splendid day he would walk part of the way, maybe all the way, down to Sloane's.

"He'll probably walk as far as the corner of Sixty-second Street and then wait for the trolley," Mamma said with a little smile as we lingered over the breakfast table. "Even when he was a young man he never looked favorably on exercise of any kind. Even so, he cannot be considered a lazy man; it's just that he likes his comfort and ease."

Yes, I thought, and when his comfort and ease are disturbed the whole household suffers. I didn't say it, though; she knew it as well as I did.

It would have been pleasant sitting at the comfortable old table with her over my second cup of coffee if I hadn't had so much on my mind, and if, every time I looked up, my glance had not fallen on the areaway steps just outside the large barred window. In spite of the fresh morning brightness I kept seeing a dark, shadowy figure, half obscured by snow, standing behind Katie and the children, and remembering how quickly it had disappeared.

"Which dress will you wear for your luncheon, Grace? And will you put on your lavaliere?"

So she had noticed. Come to think of it, there wasn't very much she did not notice.

"I think the silk paisley; it has soft enough colors to set off the amethysts, and the right neckline, too."

"In that case you'd better wear your fur coat. A cloth

coat and a silk dress simply will not do on a cold day like today. You'll look lovely, my dear. Ned will be proud of you. And don't hurry home—oh, dear, speaking of hurrying, I'd better get up to Rose. Since your father is out I can spend the morning with her. Grace, do go up to her for a few minutes while I see Cook about the grocery order."

A month had gone by since Rose's return, a long, long month, and I could see no change in her, for better or worse. In spite of Cook's efforts to "fatten her up," she was still painfully thin, and the lacklustrous eyes revealed nothing, nothing whatsoever. When I told her I was going out and asked if there was anything, a book, a magazine, or whatever, that she would like, she merely shook her head. I sat with her until Mamma came in with her workbasket and looked expectantly at Rose, hoping, I suppose, for some sign of improvement. Seeing none, she sighed and sat down heavily in the rocking chair.

I felt guilty leaving them there for what would undoubtedly be a long, silent morning, and even guiltier a few hours later when I looked in on them before going out to meet Ned and found their positions unchanged. It was as bleak a picture as I have ever seen. My mother made an effort to hide the despair in her eyes when she said goodbye to me, but Rose did not look up from the pattern in the carpet she appeared to be studying.

C H A P T E R

11

One of the pleasant things about living where we did, on East Sixty-fifth Street, was the choice of routes we had when heading downtown, to a movie, to the library on Fifty-eighth Street, or even to the dentist's. When we were children we'd argue about it.

"Let's take Madison today." (Alfred)

"It's Lexington's turn." (Grace)

"I vote for Third and the El." (Tom or Will)

"Oh, Park is more elegant." (Rose)

"Not Fifth again—it has no shops above Fifty-ninth Street." (Carrie)

And then we'd draw lots.

I chose the sunny, west side of Park Avenue that morning, thinking there would be fewer distractions there than on the busier streets. I wanted to put my thoughts in order, prepare a coherent account of the series of disturbing events of the past few days to present to Ned. By the time I reached Fifty-ninth Street, I had decided that the best thing to do was to show him the notes I had made on Christmas Eve and to tell him about the figure in the snow and the hand on my shoulder. I knew that he, unlike Alfred, would take me seriously, and I also knew that he would do everything in his power to help me.

I was a little early for our appointment, so instead of turning west toward the Plaza, I recrossed Park and walked to Lewiston's Bookstore in the hope of seeing Ann and making arrangements to speak to her privately after dinner. I had finally decided that it would be unfair not to tell her what I knew. Perhaps, in view of what happened later, though, it was just as well that she was out to lunch. The clerk told me she had asked for extra time for a special errand of some sort. I browsed for a while, lingering over the tables of secondhand books that had been set up outside the store, but she did not return. As I said, maybe it was just as well.

Ned surprised me by announcing that not only were we to have a sinfully long lunch, but also that he was taking the afternoon off and spending it with me driving through the park in one of the hansom cabs that always stood ready in front of the hotel. And it was during the slow progress along the quiet roads of Central Park that he again asked me to marry him. We must have gone about halfway around the park when he suddenly turned to me.

"I have to ask you once more, Grace. I can't wait any longer. Will you have me? When I saw you were wearing the amethysts I thought . . . look at me, Grace."

He put his hand under my chin and turned my face toward him. His eyes lighted up when he saw me nod; then his arms were around me and his lips were pressed on mine.

"Oh, my darling, my darling," he murmured, holding me close to him. "I can't believe it, I can't. You did say yes, didn't you? Say it again, love, say it again!"

We wouldn't, he said between kisses, under any circumstances, live with Mrs. Cochrane (I had momentarily forgotten about that). We would have a house of our own, or an apartment, or anything I wanted. We would have a glorious honeymoon in Venice, Paris, Rome, or even Tahiti; he couldn't stop making plans. Then after a while we were quiet; I leaned up against him, my head on his shoulder, happier than I had been in years.

So it wasn't until we alighted from the hansom cab and started walking up Fifth Avenue that I told him what had been going on at home. He made me sit down with him on one of the park benches while he read my scanty notes. Then he asked me to tell him again about the figure in the snow and the storeroom incident.

"You know, darling," he said with a frown, "it did not begin on December 23rd with those footsteps; it began that rainy night in August when someone tried to enter the house. There's a connection—"

He was not so much concerned with solving the mystery as he was with my safety, and he made all sorts of wild suggestions, like eloping immediately, taking a room at the Plaza for me, or moving me into the Cochrane house. I finally convinced him that I had a serious obligation to my parents, and he reluctantly agreed to take me home, provided I promised to barricade my door at night and never go up to the top floor again.

The reaction at home to the news of our engagement was all anyone could have desired. Mamma cried quite unashamedly, and even Papa became a little misty-eyed. He brought out his best Scotch whiskey, congratulated Ned at least a dozen times, and beamed at everyone. Ned was made to stay for dinner, the gayest meal we'd had since Thanksgiving, with everyone in fine spirits, at least everyone but Cook, who was furious she hadn't been given time to come up with something grand.

"We'll have a real engagement party," Papa said, "as soon as possible—next week—"

"Oh, please, James, give us time," Mamma broke in. "We'll have to get the back parlor ready, flowers, the caterer—"

"Mamma, no," I said. "If you don't let Cook do it all, she'll never speak to any of us again. And we don't want a lot of fuss, do we, Ned?"

"I just want what you want, love."

Under cover of the noisy general conversation, Alfred, who was sitting next to me, said he had seen Mr. Hastings downtown that afternoon.

"It's a funny thing, Grace, that I happened to run into him today of all days. No, don't look frightened; it's all right. He'd just heard from the Graves Registration people that they've identified Ben's body. He said he'd let you know, but I said I'd tell you. I meant to as soon as I came in, but with all the excitement—"

Strangely enough I felt no surprise, or disappointment, or relief from not knowing. Alfred's news was merely a confirmation of what I had suspected for a long time. I would write to Mrs. Hastings in the morning, I thought, and then wondered if she would think it unseemly if my engagement to Ned were announced in the near future. How fearful we were of the proprieties then!

In the meantime the chatter continued:

"When is the wedding to be?"

"As soon as possible!"

"And the ring?"

"We'll go to Tiffany's tomorrow."

"How many bridesmaids?"

"I want Alfred for best man."

"You'll need a ring-bearer; Carrie's youngest, perhaps."

"The lavaliere did it, Ned."

They were all genuinely happy for me, more than happy—they were delighted. Even Mamma seemed to have forgotten Rose for a while. I hoped she wouldn't remember that Rose was once to have been my maid of honor.

I don't know how long we were at the table that night, but I do remember that it was an unhurried meal, and that we did justice to the Burgundy Papa served. And I know I had nearly finished my demitasse when we heard the scream, the thumping, and the crash of breaking china. It came from above, not from the kitchen, and Ann, who could move like lightning, was the first to rush out of the dining room up the dark stairs.

Alfred, Ned, and I were close behind her, and as we arrived in the front hall I heard her cry out.

"Thank God the boys are away! Grace, don't let your mother see this!"

But it was too late: Mamma pushed me aside and stared down at Katie's body lying at the foot of the stairs amidst the shards of glass and china, her head bent at an unnatural angle. Her bright blue Irish eyes were wide open, and her mouth, which such a short time ago had been smiling happily at me, was twisted into a fierce grimace.

And Rose was standing at the top of the stairs looking down at us.

12

We were up for the rest of the night, waiting for the doctor and the undertaker. Someone, Papa, I believe, took my mother into the front parlor and made her sit well back in a corner, out of sight of the activity in the hall. Later, much later, when poor Katie's body had been removed, Alfred and Ned half guided, half carried her upstairs to her room. Dr. Bronson administered a sedative before he left and said to keep her in bed for the next few days.

At three in the morning, the four of us, Ned, Alfred, Ann, and I gathered in the front parlor, exhausted, but unwilling to go to bed. We went over everything that had taken place, and when I told my brother and his wife what had happened when I was looking for the footstool Alfred finally agreed that the footsteps Ann and I had heard might have been real.

Ann blanched when she heard about the hand on my shoulder; she sat huddled up against Alfred, trying to control the quivering muscles around her mouth and holding her hands tightly clasped to prevent their trembling.

"There's obviously someone in the house who doesn't belong here," Ned said, "and we'd better find him."

"But where could anyone hide for days on end?" Alfred asked. "Say he got in the day I found the areaway door open—wasn't that just before Christmas, Grace? Yes, the 23rd, and today's the 27th—no, by now it's the 28th—"

"He must be up on the top floor—"

"Where? In the storeroom?"

"It must have been his hand; maybe he meant to push me down the stairs."

"And then he heard Katie coming?"

"You mean he could have pushed Katie? She didn't trip?"

"Katie was the one who found me; he may have thought she had seen him."

"I think," Alfred said slowly, "that Katie knew those stairs like the palm of her hand. I think someone pushed or tripped her. And I think Ned and I should go up to the fifth floor at once. Where are Cook and Maggie?"

"Down in the kitchen; they wouldn't go to bed."

Alfred gently removed his arm from around Ann's shoulders and stood up. Ned kissed me quickly, quickly but hard, and they left us.

"What is going to happen, Grace?" Ann whispered.

"I wish I knew. There seems to be no end in sight; Rose, Katie, Mamma, footsteps—can anything else go wrong?"

"Pretty soon, I hope, Alfred and I will be able to afford an apartment—"

That's all very well for you, I thought. You can get out; I don't see how I can. How can I leave Papa with two invalids and a crazy, unknown person in the house?

"Grace, you ought to marry Ned at once and go away quickly before anything else happens."

"Ann, I don't see how I can even go back to school after the holidays; someone must take charge here."

We talked in a desultory way about Rose's condition, Mamma's health, the possibility of hiring a nurse or housekeeper, the necessity of finding a replacement for Katie, and I don't know what else. Then we were quiet, tired of coming to no conclusions, and waited for the men to return.

"There's no one up there now," Alfred said. "We forced the storeroom door and looked in; nothing but boxes of old stuff, a few lamps and pictures, you know, worthless junk."

"What about the bedrooms up there?"

"We went over each one, closets and all, and the bathroom, even the laundry hamper."

So nothing was accomplished that night. Ned went home to get a few hours' sleep before going to the office, and I went up to lie on my bed, wide awake and miserable. I don't know about Alfred and Ann.

The first thing I did the next morning was to call Dr. Bronson and enlist his help in persuading my father that we needed a nurse, one who could both care for Mamma and keep an eye on Rose. He fully agreed with me and said he would be over in the early afternoon. Then I went down to the kitchen to talk to Cook and Maggie. Thank goodness they had no idea that Katie's death was anything but an accident; they were obviously grieving, but they were not frightened. I told them I would arrange for a funeral Mass at St. Vincent Ferrer's church on Sixty-sixth Street and see about a burial plot in Calvary Cemetery in Queens.

"And I'll have to interview someone to help you, Maggie. I'll call the agency as soon as I go upstairs."

"Oh, Miss Grace, wait. I know a girl, a sort of cousin, distant, you might say, name of Lizzie McCabe. Could you be seein' her?"

Cook nodded. Apparently she knew Lizzie McCabe and approved.

"Bless you, Maggie. Send her to see me as soon as you can. And could you, would you collect Katie's things? Did she have any relatives?"

"No one, Miss Grace, no one at all. Katie was alone in this world. May she not be alone in the next one, God rest her soul."

I began to think maybe I would be able to go back to school; it might be possible if Lizzie McCabe and the nurse worked out. At the time I wasn't as enchanted with teaching as I was later, when I became a full professor, but the work was rewarding, and besides, I needed it.

Papa's main objection to having a nurse was that he would have to give up his bed to her. Where would he sleep? In the back parlor? On the floor? How would you feel, Grace, if you were put out of your room? (Obviously he had forgotten that I had been forced out of my comfortable quarters.) The self-centeredness of old age is something I must guard against, but it's difficult when one lives alone.

When I reminded my father that we'd had a nurse for Mamma in East Quogue, he said that was an entirely different situation and not relevant. But in the end he had to give in; Dr. Bronson convinced him that there was no alternative to professional care, and that we would need both day and night nurses.

"You mean I'm to have a strange woman sitting up all night in my bedroom—or lying on my bed? What about me? No, absolutely no! I won't stand for it. It's immoral, that's what it is."

"Of course not, Mr. Millerton," the doctor said. "The night nurse can stay in Rose's room when she's not needed by Mrs. Millerton, and as for the day nurse, well, you are not up in the bedroom then anyway. She won't interfere with you at all. You want your wife to have every consideration and comfort, don't you?"

It took a while, but in the end Papa grudgingly consented, and a Miss Pomfret arrived at eight that night. A Miss Twigg took over at eight the next morning (what long hours those women worked!), and both of them, either instinctively or on the advice of Dr. Bronson, steered clear of my father.

In spite of the extra help (Lizzie McCabe was settling in nicely under Maggie's tutelage) I was unable to relax; the picture of Katie's broken body at the foot of the stairs haunted me, and it seemed as if a hand were never very far from my shoulder. I was not the only one whose nerves were on edge; Alfred and Ann were at odds, bickering over trifles, and once in a while I heard raised voices behind their closed door. Papa wasn't edgy; he was simply morose. Rose would have nothing to do with either of the nurses. They told me she sat with her back to them whenever they were in her room, and said "go away" if they went near her.

Another picture haunted me, that of Rose standing at the top of the stairs looking down at Katie. We had all assumed that the noise of the crash had brought her out of her room, but had it? She could have pushed

Katie off the top step. She was strong enough—I thought of what Ned had said about the strength of the weak—and her mind was not what I would call sound. Cook said her appetite had fallen off, too; since Katie's death, her trays were going back to the kitchen with half the food uneaten. I couldn't explain it, although I wondered if she were yearning for Mamma, in a reversion to childhood.

In all the excitement my engagement had been virtually forgotten by everyone, except for Mrs. Cochrane, who wrote me a most effusive congratulatory note and invited me to a small New Year's Eve gathering.

I went to the party to please Ned, and although I had little desire to welcome in a new year that held forth so little promise of peace of mind, I did enjoy myself. I didn't have time to buy a new dress, and that rather bothered me. That winter the evening gowns were unusually elaborate: rich fabrics trimmed with gold lace and intricate embroidery in beads and sequins were all the rage, and I was amused to note that most of the New Year's Eve guests, even members of the most conservative New York families, had succumbed to the fashion.

Mrs. Cochrane herself was resplendent in floor-length black velvet figured in gold and silver thread and with wide, black chiffon sleeves. At first I felt rather underdressed in my white crepe de chine, whose only adornment was a pair of satin panels that hung down from the shoulders in back. But I knew it was a becoming dress and didn't worry about its simplicity once the party was under way.

Ned's mother, accomplished hostess that she was, had made up her guest list with care and invited a number of Ned's and my friends along with several of her own generation. At midnight we sat down to a beautifully appointed champagne supper at which the newly engaged couple was toasted with decorous enthusiasm. I think some thought it queer that I had as yet no ring, and that we had not set a date for the wedding, but they were all too well bred to ask why.

I thought Ned must have told his mother something about the situation at home, because after inquiring about my parents' health she asked about my sister.

"And Rose, the little beauty? Is she getting over Egerton? By the way, Grace, how well did you know him?"

"Not well at all. They eloped shortly after she met him, you know."

"Well, his reputation leaves something to be desired. He was not at all welcome in Remsenberg. I wish I'd known—I could have warned you. But I never had any idea he was in East Quogue that summer. Perhaps his disappearance is a blessing in disguise, my dear. Rose will get over him in time."

In the cab on the way home I asked Ned how much his mother knew about what had been going on in our house.

"Nothing, absolutely nothing," he replied. "It is none of her concern, and I wouldn't think of mentioning it to her. And I'm sorry, love, that she questioned you about Rose. That does not concern her, either. I suppose the gossip grapevine has been busy."

Then he held me close to him until the cab drew up in front of the house.

"Do you want me to come in with you, to see—"

"Oh, Ned, I'd dearly love to have you come all the way up to the fourth floor with me—no, that's silly; the night nurse will be on duty, and I'll check with her."

He saw me safely inside the front door, and after kissing me goodnight over and over again and saying he'd see me the following afternoon, he left. Rose's door was closed, but Mamma's was open partially, and I could see Miss Pomfret sitting next to the bed. She came out into the hall when she saw me, saying that my mother had seemed restless earlier in the night and she thought it best to stay at her side.

"Mr. Millerton is so sound asleep, he'll never know. And I'll slip out early, before he wakes up."

"And Rose?" I asked.

"She made it very clear she wanted to be alone in her room. I think she went to sleep early; I've heard no sound from her." And after wishing me a Happy New Year she went back to her patient.

13

By the middle of January things began to look better: I was back at school, the little boys were home, Mamma was making a good recovery from what we now knew had been a mild heart attack, and the day nurse had been let go. I had succeeded in convincing myself that Katie had tripped, that the hand on my shoulder must have been hers, that there were no footsteps, and that the figure in the snow was simply that of an ordinary passerby.

I was seeing Ned almost daily; if he didn't take me out to dinner, which he did two or three times a week, he came to see me in the evening. The engagement ring he bought caused no little comment. Instead of the traditional diamond, he ordered an emerald set with small diamonds, a most unusual choice, and one very much to my liking. We decided on a June wedding so that I could finish out the term at school, and I planned to take a year's leave of absence, after which I would see if I wanted to continue teaching or not. We settled on Switzerland for a honeymoon; Ned had once stayed at a small hotel on Lake Geneva that he wanted me to see. And we started looking for a place to live.

Now that she was better, Mamma took a keen interest in all of our plans and liked having Ned and me sit with her for a short time in the evening discussing them.

"As soon as I'm allowed to go abroad, Grace, we'll see to your clothes. You'll need so many things. Oh, I almost forgot to tell you, but Dr. Bronson said that beginning next week we won't need Miss Pomfret. Your father is *very* pleased! He said he guessed he could stand her for another six nights."

I had been out so much (and what a relief that was!) with Ned and at school that I hadn't seen the doctor since the beginning of the month and made a mental note to talk to him. I hadn't seen very much of Alfred and Ann, either, so one evening after Ned left early I went up to ask them if they'd like some cake or cookies before going to bed. Their door was closed, and I was about to knock when I heard Alfred shout.

"You sold it, didn't you? And where, may I ask, is the money?"

"Hush! Stop it! Someone will hear you!"

"What did you do with it? Tell me, damn it!"

"You're hurting me! Stop! I had to have it, that's all. No, Alfred—I have it! I'll scream—"

Then there was silence.

It was certainly no time to ask them if they wanted something to eat, so I slipped off my shoes and tiptoed down the hall to my own room.

Remembering our conversation about Tiffany's on Christmas day, I felt certain that it was the diamond pin she had sold. But why? Ned had told me a few days earlier that they were doing nicely, making regular payments on the loan and incurring no debts that he knew of. And Ann had talked about being able to afford an apartment soon; perhaps that was what she wanted the money for. Or did Alfred need it? Had he lied to me about Ann's annuity? Had she?

The next day, Tuesday, I had to be at school earlier than usual, for a conference, and left the house before they came down for breakfast. So it wasn't until almost six in the evening that I saw Ann. I was in my room, hearing Charles' spelling words (he was to be in a spelling bee the next day), when she came in from the bookstore. She looked exhausted, and merely gave us a tired wave before going into her room.

"Deceive, d-e-c-e-i-v-e, deceive," chanted Charles. "'I' before 'e' except after 'c'—"

A muffled scream came from the back bedroom, followed by hysterical laughter, horrible, dreadful sounds. By the time I got there, Ann was sitting on the floor, rocking back and forth, moaning and pointing to her dressing table. There, amid the bottles of scent and jars of cream lay a dead, gaping cat, not one of ours, but a wild one, a scrawny, ugly specimen such as prowled in the backyards. When I looked closely, I saw that it had been strangled with a length of picture wire.

"Rose," gasped Ann. "Rose did it."

"Rose? How could she possibly?"

"She did—I know—she knows—"

"But she won't even come out of her room! How on earth could she—what does she know?"

"She knows, she knows she did it—go ask her!"

I found Rose sitting next to the fireplace with tears streaming down her cheeks. To my amazement, she spoke before I could say a word.

"I thought it was Pumpy." That was all. I could get nothing more out of her.

"Grace, what is it? Who screamed? Is someone ill?"

I had forgotten about Mamma, who now stood in the doorway of Rose's room. I quickly made up something about Ann's having seen a mouse and thinking it was a rat. It was a feeble effort, I know, but my mother believed it. I took her back to her own room so that she wouldn't be upset by Rose's tears and then went upstairs again. Ann was in the front bedroom with the two frightened little boys, hastily stuffing clothes into a suitcase.

"I can't stand it. Too many things—we can't stay here any longer. It's not safe—"

After Alfred came home and disposed of the cat (simply by throwing it out the window and into the yard where it had once prowled), she calmed down, but she still kept talking about leaving.

"I can't face dinner tonight; tell them I have a headache. And I'll sleep in here with the boys—that room—"

"Where were you thinking of going, Ann? Surely not to your parents?" Alfred's voice was cold, his eyes hard.

"Oh, I don't know—don't bother me; go have your dinner. I'm going to take some aspirin and lie down."

I took Charles and Francis down to the front parlor, where Lizzie was setting out a tray of fruit juice and sherry. Papa had apparently not heard the disturbance—he was inclined to doze in his chair in the late afternoon—and no one mentioned the dead cat to him. Even the little boys knew better than that.

14

She must have slipped out while we were at dinner, because when we went up, the fourth floor was empty. Alfred kept calm, but his face was ashen. He sent the children to bed after I had heard the rest of Charles' spelling words, and then he and I went down to the parlor.

"Won't Ned be over tonight, Grace?" Papa asked.

"I'm afraid not. He's having dinner with a client. I don't think he relished the prospect, but it's something he had to do."

Conversation languished, and shortly after nine my father left us, saying he hoped Miss Pomfret would permit him to undress in privacy.

"If she would only tell me what she's up to," Alfred said as soon as we were alone. "Then I'd know where I stand, but I feel as if I'm going around blindfolded."

"She's had a shock, Alfred—"

"Oh, it's not just the dead cat—where in hell did that come from anyway? It's a whole series of things. You know the diamond pin she got for Christmas?

Well, it's gone. I'm convinced she sold it, and she won't say why or what's become of the money. Grace, I'm worried sick. Just when I'm getting back on my feet and beginning to see my way clear to moving into a home of our own. And where'd she go off to? She didn't take any clothes with her."

We both heard the key in the front door at the same time, and Alfred rushed into the hall to envelope Ann in a strong embrace, all anger gone in his relief at seeing her.

"You're all right?" he murmured.

"Yes, all right—for a while, I think—just needed some air; that's always good for a headache."

"Sit down with Grace. I'll see if Cook will fix you some warm milk." And he was off to the kitchen.

"The walk did me good, I think. It's pleasant out tonight; January thaw, probably."

It was obvious that she wanted the conversation to be impersonal, so when Alfred came back with three glasses of milk (fortified) we talked of nothing but trivialities until it was time for bed. Then Ann broke down again.

"I can't, can't sleep in that room!" she wailed. "The cat will be there—"

"The cat's gone, darling. I got rid of it; you saw me do it."

"No, I said no. I'll sleep on the couch in the boys' room."

"Let her sleep there, Alfred, for tonight anyway, and I'll have Maggie and Lizzie give your room an airing and a thorough cleaning tomorrow."

"The cat will always be there."

As I helped her make up the old couch in the front room, I wondered why Alfred wasn't more concerned about the cat, how it got there, who put it there, and who killed it. He had thrown it out the window, and that was the end of it—for him. I doubt that he even noticed the picture wire around the neck.

In spite of the warm milk, I could not sleep at once; I kept thinking of Rose. She couldn't possibly have caught a homeless cat, strangled it, and put it on Ann's dressing table, and yet she knew about it and was afraid it was Pumpy. There! The fact that she thought it might have been Pumpy was proof that she hadn't done it. But then, how did she know *anything* about it?

And I wondered about Ann; I didn't believe for one minute that she went out just for a breath of air. And what did she mean when she said she was all right "for a while"? She and Rose were hiding things . . .

15

The next morning I was sure that Rose was either concealing something (something recent, I mean, not her past) or living in a fantasy world. She was standing at her partially open bedroom door when I went down to breakfast. I glanced at Mamma's door, where I could see Miss Pomfret preparing to go off duty, but a glance was all I had time for, because Rose took hold of my arm, and with a show of strength that surprised me pulled me into her room, closing the door with her free hand. Her eyes, no longer vague and blank, blazed at me with a fierce intensity, and still gripping my arm, she spoke in a whisper.

"Tell Ann it is not enough."

"What on earth do you mean?"

"Tell Ann it is not enough."

"Rose, what is not enough? You're hurting my arm!"

"She knows. Tell her."

"Why don't you tell her?"

"She's gone down. I missed her."

My head was whirling. I think I even forgot to be

surprised that Rose was carrying on a conversation—if you could call it that. My mind went back to Ann's hysterical outburst the night before about Rose and the cat, but I could make no connection between that and my sister's enigmatic message.

"All right, Rose. I'll tell her, if you tell me what it means."

"No, no," and she tightened her hold on my arm. "No one else must know. Ann will know."

"Yes, all right. Please let go. You're hurting me."

"Promise?"

"Yes, let go."

I waited until the boys went off to school (sometimes we walked the three blocks together, but that morning I told them to go on ahead) and then gave Ann the message. We were in the front hall at the time. I stood with my hat and coat on, but Ann, who didn't have to be at the store until later, had half-turned to go up to her room. When I repeated what Rose had said, she immediately looked away from me, and muttering something that sounded like "What nonsense," ran upstairs. Whether she stopped on Rose's floor or went on up to her own I didn't know. I left for school, half wishing I'd never have to return to the house.

"Rose is definitely better," Papa said when I got home that afternoon. "She told your mother she'd like to go out and get some new clothes. I'd let her buy out Bloomingdale's if it would help. Have some tea, Grace, and pour me a cup, please."

"Was Dr. Bronson in today?" I asked.

"No, but I called him, and told him Rose was on the mend. He's coming first thing in the morning. I'll ask him to recommend little outings for her, walks in the park and such."

He rambled on, making plans to take Rose and Mamma away, to Atlantic City, perhaps, for some bracing sea air. I only half listened as I sat there in the comfortable, worn surroundings I had known for so long, and marvelled at how we all protected my father (and my mother, of course) from all the troublesome things that were going on. In his case, we did it in our own interest, I suppose; it was easier to keep him in the dark than to risk his irascibility.

I left him chuckling over the Fontaine Fox cartoon in *The Sun* and went up to change. Mamma was in Rose's room, all smiles as she watched my sister pinning up her hair. Rose was actually chatty, making plans to go to the hairdresser, to come down to meals, to buy some new clothes, in short, to resume living.

"I'm all better, Grace," she crowed, giving me a spontaneous hug. "All better, free. You won't have to worry about me now."

"Free of what, Rosie?"

"Free of illness, silly. What else?"

But I was not free of worry; something was unreal.

Ned took me to the Waldorf for dinner that night, and there in the old fashioned elegance of the Orangerie I brought him up to date on events in the brownstone house. He was as puzzled as I had been by Rose's message for Ann and horrified when he heard about the dead cat. He had me go over all the details again, just as I have written them here, and did not speak until I finished.

"Grace, dear, I don't like it; there's something dangerous going on, and I'm worried about you. I don't think you can take much more of this, darling. I know Rose is your sister and that family ties are strong, but she isn't normal. We don't know that she didn't push

Katie down the stairs, and we don't know what she does all day while she's so much alone. She ought to be institutionalized; a diseased mind, capable of plotting horrors—"

"But Ned, she was so much better this afternoon—"

"Yes, but didn't Bronson say schizophrenia has phases? This may not last; I don't think it means she's cured. You say she surprised you with her strength this morning; she's probably strong enough to strangle a cat—a maniacal strength, if you will. And she might just as well have put the cat in your room instead of Ann's. She's crazy, Grace, and you can't tell what she'll do next. Keep away from her, love. God, I wish I could get you out of there for good. Look, Grace, why can't we be married before June?"

By the time we finished dinner, I had agreed not only to go house hunting with him the coming Saturday, but also to marry him as soon as we found a place to live. I was just as anxious as he was to get settled, and, more than anything, I wanted to get away from the smothering atmosphere of the brownstone house.

It was still early when we left the Waldorf, and since I was in no hurry to go home I asked Ned to take me to see a movie.

"I know just the one," he said. "*The Hunchback of Notre Dame* is playing at the Plaza, and they say Lon Chaney is great as Quasimodo. Would you like that?"

I did like it, immensely.

The next night, Thursday, was something of a celebration. Mamma came downstairs for the first time since the Christmas holidays, and sitting comfortably next to the fire with her small feet resting on the new footstool, she looked like someone in an old daguerreotype. Rose, when she appeared at the dinner table, was given a round of applause, and when Ned came in later we were all up in the parlor sipping the brandy Papa had brought out in honor of the occasion. I thought my father rather overdid the genial host routine, but no one else seemed to mind. Rose complained, but only mildly, that the doctor wouldn't permit her to go out for a few days and chattered on about all the things she wanted to do. Except for an unnatural brightness in her eyes, she seemed perfectly normal, but the change had been so radical, and Ned had been so skeptical about any real cure, that I felt uneasy. She greeted Ned warmly, congratulated him on our engagement, and asked about the wedding plans.

"June 30th," he responded with a glance at me, "then off to an Alpine lake for six weeks. That's all I know at the moment. Except that Grace and I are going house hunting on Saturday."

From then on the conversation centered on living quarters, the advantages of an apartment over a town house, the most desirable neighborhood, that sort of thing. It wasn't late, only about nine-thirty, when Miss Pomfret came in to take my mother up to bed.

"And Rose, you'd better come too," Mamma said. "It's your first day downstairs, you know."

"Oh, not yet, Mamma—"

"ROSE!" The command in Papa's voice was unmistakable. Rose turned and followed the nurse and my mother out of the room without another word.

Ann, who had been rather quiet all evening, turned to Papa.

"Mr. Millerton, was Dr. Bronson able to account for the change in Rose?"

"He said, my dear, that no one can fully explain things like this. Something clicked into place, was how he put it, and we should be grateful. And we're to keep a close watch on her and see that she doesn't overdo. That's why I sent her up just now."

"Her eyes looked funny to me," Alfred said. "Sort of glittery."

"Nonsense, my boy. Just the result of the medicine, that's all."

"I don't think that is all, Mr. Millerton," Ann said, getting up from her chair. "There are too many things we don't know about Rose: where was she for four years? What kind of life did she lead that brought on her illness?"

"Ann raises some good questions," Alfred said quickly, before Papa could reply. "And only Rose can answer them. I suggest we ask her."

"NO!" thundered my father. "You are not to question the child. That's an order."

The celebratory mood of the earlier part of the evening was completely dispelled, and it wasn't long before the others went up to bed, leaving Ned and me alone. The moment they were gone his arms went around me, and we had a quiet half hour to ourselves. When I went upstairs, all the bedroom doors were closed but mine. I had no way of knowing whether Ann was in her own bed or on the couch in the boys' room.

16

We looked at three apartments on Saturday afternoon. Neither of us liked the first two, but the third, which was spacious and well laid out, overlooked the park and appealed to us both. We had agreed, however, to look at some houses the following week, so we made no immediate decision. My own preference would have been for an apartment; I'd had enough of long flights of dark stairs and dim hallways. But then, Ned and I had always lived in houses, winter and summer, and I wondered whether we would find life all on one floor too confining.

"We'd never get a view like that from a house, love," he said as we walked up Fifth Avenue toward the Metropolitan Museum. And of course he was right; the only views we'd ever had were of Sixty-fifth Street from the front and the backs of houses from the rear.

I mustn't spend too much time on this part (although I do enjoy remembering that afternoon). Suffice it to say that we retraced our steps to the apartment, put a deposit down on it, and made arrangements to sign a lease. It was too late in the day to start looking for furniture, so we wandered through the main picture galleries of the museum—it was never crowded in those days, even on a Saturday—and ended up in a large hall containing exquisite models of the great cathedrals of Europe. Two little girls, eight or nine years old, I suppose, were examining the replica of Notre Dame, and as we paused to watch them the younger of the two pointed to a certain spot on the structure.

"There it is," she cried. "That's where the hunchback climbed, right there."

"And she's dead right," Ned said with a chuckle. "There's someone else who'll never forget Lon Chaney."

The children, evidently embarrassed at having attracted attention, giggled and ran behind the model of a Greek temple. Just then, as we were turning away from the exhibit, I caught sight of a man walking rapidly out of the room we were in. It was not only the long stride with which he walked that attracted my attention—no one hurries in museums—but also his build, which was tall, slender, and vaguely familiar. He was gone in a minute, but not before I realized that he reminded me of the man I had seen clinging to the railing at the Astor house last summer—but then I thought I was being foolish, and decided to say nothing to Ned.

It was windy and cold when we emerged from the museum, and as we stood waiting for a taxi a few flakes of snow blew in our faces.

"Well, what do you think, love?" Ned asked as the cab made its way down Fifth Avenue. "Do you still want to go to the opera tonight?" Mrs. Cochrane, who was visiting friends in Miami, had offered us the use of her box while she was gone. "Or does an evening in front of the fire have more appeal?"

"If we could be alone it would, but with the whole family there . . . Ned dear, I don't know what's happening to me; I'm tired of listening to them, tired of worrying about them, and I—I'm beginning to hate that house."

"We could go to my house, love. Mrs. Brady will rustle up some food for us; she and Brady manage without the rest of the help when I'm there alone . . ." and he leaned forward to tell the driver to go on down to Forty-ninth Street.

"Oh, Ned, do you think—"

"Of course I think. Now put your head on my shoulder—there."

It was snowing hard by the time we ran up the steps of the Cochrane house, and I welcomed the prospect of the promised fire. Ned let us in with his key, and a dark-coated manservant appeared almost immediately to take our damp coats.

"Ah, Brady, there you are. Light a fire in my study, will you? And then bring up some ice, if you will."

"Ice, Mr. Ned? On a night like this? Not something hot?"

"Yes, ice, Brady. We need something stronger than tea tonight."

I had never been in Ned's study before and was surprised at the contrast between it and the other rooms on the first floor, what we used to call the "public rooms." It was really too big for a study (it had once been his father's library), but in spite of its size it exuded an air of informality and comfort, so lacking in Mrs. Cochrane's sitting rooms. A large, deep, leather sofa was drawn up conveniently in front of the fireplace, and once the logs caught, the light of the flames picked out the bright colors of the oriental rug that covered most of the floor. Two of the four walls were given over to bookshelves that reached up to the high ceiling, and as Brady went around turning on the reading lamps and drawing the crimson drapes across the windows, the warmth and coziness became almost palpable. Books and periodicals were scattered about on tables next to big leather armchairs as well as on the long library table behind the sofa, and the chair in front of the desk near one of the windows looked as if Ned had just pushed it back and risen from it. Comfortable disorder, I thought to myself.

I could feel his eyes on me as I looked around the room, and thought he was waiting to hear my reaction to it. He wasn't at all; he was waiting for Brady to leave so that he could take me in his arms. After a while I reminded him of the drinks he had mixed and left on the shelf near the fireplace, which was just as well, because as he got up from the sofa Brady appeared with a tray of toasted cheese canapés and a query about dinner.

"Mrs. Brady would like to know, Mr. Ned, if you would prefer the small dining room tonight?"

"By all means. And tell Mrs. Brady we'd like dinner at seven if she can manage it."

"That she can, sir, I'm sure. And which wine will you be wanting? It's some kind of chicken she's preparing."

"The Moselle, I think, thank you."

Brady left, and as we sat watching the fire and savoring our drinks we talked about how we would furnish the apartment. There would be a library-study there, too, and I was saying something about having the same kind of drapes in it when Ned interrupted me.

"Darling," he said, putting his hand under my chin and tilting my face up to his, "we'll have anything you want, and we'll talk about whatever you like from now through dinner. Afterward—"

"After dinner, you mean? What—"

"After dinner I'll want the rest of the evening to tell you how much I love you."

Mrs. Brady provided us with a subtly flavored chicken-and-rice dish, which was accompanied by a salad and tiny rolls that rivalled in lightness and texture any Cook ever made. While we were eating the dessert, warm gingerbread with a fruit sauce, Ned ordered coffee and brandy to be served up in the study and asked Brady to supply some more wood for the fire . . .

It was still snowing when he took me home around midnight, but the wind had died down, and the city streets had an unusually quiet, peaceful appearance. The cab driver, a pleasant young man, told us that a foot or more of snow was expected by morning.

"Good thing it's Sunday," he said. "At least for them as doesn't have to work. Make a lazy day of it, they can, laying around looking out the window at the snow." In spite of this somewhat grumbling remark, he sounded almost cheerful, either from the excitement a big storm often generates or from the prospect of extra fares the next day.

Ned asked him to wait and helped me struggle up the snow-covered steps of the stoop. Before I could put my key in the door an excited Miss Pomfret flung it open.

"I've been watching for you from the parlor window, Miss Millerton. Your father's been frantic with worry about you, you not being here for dinner and all—and that's not all: I've been going up to check on Mrs. Millerton—they're both asleep now—and I heard voices in Rose's room—"

"Perhaps Ann is with her," I said.

"No, no, it didn't sound like her. Sort of a hoarse, low voice—and she's locked herself in, and just says to go away when I knock."

"Could you hear what she was saying?" Ned asked.

"Not at all; it was too low. But it was her voice, and then the other one, sort of like someone with laryngitis."

"Ned—"

"Of course, love. No, let me go first, Miss Pomfret."

Nothing came of it. The three of us stood in the silent, dimly lit hall outside Rose's door for a good five minutes and heard no sound. I remembered that the bathroom door to her room locked only on the bath side and asked the nurse if she had tried that.

"Yes," she nodded. "She has something pushed up against it. What can she be up to? I feel responsible, you know, having been asked to keep an eye on her. And even if she is so much better—"

Short of breaking down the door and waking the entire household, there didn't seem to be anything we could do. Miss Pomfret went back to my parents' room, muttering that she was glad she had only one more night of this, and I went downstairs to see Ned out.

He started to say goodnight, but I clung to him so that he changed his mind.

"Wait in the parlor, love, while I pay off the taxi. I'll be right there."

A few minutes later I was in his arms again, and for a while I forgot about everything in the world but the tender strength of his love. A dull, gray dawn was breaking over the snow-covered city when he left me, promising to return in the late afternoon. I went slowly up the stairs, past all the closed doors, to my room, where I sat at the window for some time before I slept.

17

"Of course there was no one in my room," Rose said angrily. "And what if I did lock my door? I can't stand that Pomfret woman snooping around. I've a right to some privacy."

She and I were in her room the next afternoon. Mamma was taking a nap; Alfred and Ann had taken Francis to the park for some sleigh riding; Charles, who was home with a cold, was playing rummy with Papa in the parlor, and Ned had not yet arrived.

"And you barricaded the door to the bathroom—"

"And why not, pray? I didn't want her coming in that way, did I?"

"Aunt Grace, Ned's here," Charles called from below.

"Uncle Ned to you, fellow," I heard him say. "A little respect for your elders, if you please. Ah, Grace—"

"Are you going out? Can't you play a game of backgammon with us?"

"We are going out, to a gorgeous tea at the Plaza, aren't we, Ned?"

"We are indeed. But maybe later on, Charles, we'll challenge you to a game."

A piercing scream came from the floor above, startling us all. When we got there, Ned, my father, Charles, and I, we saw Rose bending over my mother, who lay on the floor of the bathroom next to the tub, with her head up against its wooden casing. Mamma gestured weakly in the direction of the toilet compartment and tried to speak, but only a terrible sound came from her, a combination of a croak and a groan. She died a few minutes later.

Because of the shock, no doubt, I do not recall every last detail of the events that followed immediately after my mother's death, but some things I do remember clearly: Papa went into his room, closing the door softly behind him; Ned took Charles downstairs and stayed with him until Alfred and Ann brought Francis home; I sent Rose for a quilt, and when we had covered the body, she straightened up, murmuring to herself.

"Well, at least we don't need the Pomfret woman tonight."

"Rose, for pity's sake!"

"I'm sorry, Grace, I only meant—"

"I don't care what you meant! Go down and ask Ned to phone the doctor—oh, never mind, here's Alfred. Alfred, we must let Carrie and Tom and Will know—"

There was so much to be done, so many arrangements to be made, that I forgot about Rose until late in the evening. We had had an almost silent meal; Papa did not come down, and poor Charles ate hardly anything. Afterward, when we were all in the parlor going over a list Alfred had made of things to be done, I caught sight of her as she slipped out of the room and went slowly up the stairs. She looked like a sleepwalker.

We got through the next few days somehow, the wake, the funeral and all. The infrequent moments I could snatch with Ned were my only comfort. Papa had retired into himself, and paradoxically, in being completely undemanding was more demanding than ever, in that he aroused such concern. And Rose was bothering me; she was so quiet that I was afraid she was becoming ill again, reverting to her state of disinterest and vagueness. Her eyes were not expressionless, however, and I attributed her passivity to shock caused by witnessing Mamma's death. When I spoke to Dr. Bronson about her, he agreed that this might very well be the case.

"Give her time, Grace. She'll probably come out of it again. An occasional fit of depression is not significant, but let me know if it continues for any length of time."

Alfred and Ann went back to work, but I kept postponing my return to school. I hated to leave my father and sister to themselves for the greater part of the day, even though I didn't seem to be doing either of them any good. What with Rose mooning around like a lost soul and Papa sitting dispiritedly in the parlor all day long, the atmosphere in the house was heavy. Even Cook was out of sorts, as evidenced by the fact that she gave us the same dinner two nights in a row. As for me, I felt trapped; I couldn't leave, and I couldn't stay. I don't know how long this state of affairs might have lasted if Carrie hadn't read me a lecture. She came over one afternoon to go through Mamma's personal things with me (Papa would have nothing to do with that) and while we sorted the clothing she urged me not to give up teaching.

"And what about Ned, Grace? You should be devoting yourself to him, not to Papa and Rose. Both of them will take and take and take, and give you nothing in return."

"But left to themselves, Carrie?"

"Nonsense. They think only of themselves as it is, so it makes no difference. You should get out; you wouldn't even need a housekeeper. Cook has been running this house for years; you can leave everything to her. I know we always gave Mamma all the credit for managing things, but she really did very little. She knew how to train servants and how to keep them; after that, she could just sit back. That was enough for her, Grace, but it would never be enough for you, and if you're not careful that's the position you'll find yourself in. Alfred and Ann will move out, and you will be at the beck and call of a selfish old man and an irrational, equally selfish girl. Here, what shall we do with the silver dresser set?

"Oh, my," she said with a laugh, "I remember so well sitting right here, fiddling with this buttonhook, while Mamma gave me her vague version of what menstruation was. She hadn't prepared me for it at all, and when it happened I was terrified, thought I had some dreadful disease and was bleeding to death. She was so reluctant to talk about it that I ended up thinking it was something that occurred only in our family! Can you believe that? I used to sit in school and look around at the other girls in the class, envying them because they were free of it."

"Carrie, how awful for you! But you were so good with Rose and me later on. Did you know that Mamma never once mentioned menstruation to either of us? When I told her it had happened she just nodded and changed the subject—it was completely unmention-able. Thank goodness you warned me."

"And thank goodness I married a doctor, Grace. John was horrified at my innocence; really, he had to tell me everything about sex. He couldn't believe how ignorant I was, said it wasn't healthy, and could ruin our lives. Maybe it did ruin Rose's—"

She picked up a pair of Mamma's soft French kid gloves and folded them carefully before going on.

"Don't be shy with Ned, Grace. Underneath that handsome, calm exterior he's a passionate man, or I miss my guess. And of course he's absolutely mad about you. Talk to him about everything, Grace, ask him about things, and let him teach you—"

She broke off and hugged me when she saw that I was smiling.

"Oh, Grace dear, it's so good to see you really in love; I never thought it was the real thing with Ben Hastings. Now, take my advice, and get out from un-der Papa's thumb, and quickly. Understand?"

Carrie's forthright lecture had its effect: after she left, I called Ned at his office and made arrangements to meet him for dinner. The delight in his voice was heartwarming and did a world of good for my flagging spirits.

"Are you sure you don't want me to pick you up, darling?" he asked.

"No, thank you, Ned; that takes up too much time."

"And we've had little enough of that lately. All right, love, I'll meet you at six at Ricardo's."

I knew it was possible that Papa had overheard the conversation on account of the unfortunate position of the telephone, but he'd been so disinterested in every-thing lately that I doubted that he'd actually listened. I was wrong.

"Grace!" he called from the parlor. "Do you really think it advisable to be going out to dinner so soon? Tell Ned to come here, if you must see him. It would look better, much better."

I almost acquiesced, but Carrie's warning was too fresh in my mind.

"No, Papa," I said as gently as I could. "Ned and I have things to discuss privately."

"Well, couldn't you discuss them under your own roof? Do you have to go to some crowded restaurant where you're sure to be seen? And probably over-heard?"

When I made no reply he picked up his newspaper and opened it so that his face was hidden. I was half-way out of the room when he spoke again.

"Very well, very well, go your own way. Don't pay any attention to me. But don't blame me if there's talk. And take that damn footstool out of here, will you?"

I changed from the black wool dress I had been wearing almost constantly since the funeral into a soft gray Jacquard silk (perfect with the lavaliere) and was careful to button up my fur coat so Papa wouldn't notice. He probably wouldn't have, but if he had it would have been just one more thing that might cause "talk."

Ned was waiting at the restaurant, where he had reserved one of the more secluded tables in the rear, and over dinner I gave him the gist of Carrie's lecture, omitting the part about menstruation, of course.

"I couldn't agree more heartily, Grace dear. I think you should go back to school if that's what you want, and I also think we should be married quietly, as soon as possible. If you'd like to postpone the honeymoon—we'd planned it for the summer, anyway—all we have to do is finish furnishing the apartment. The decorators should be through by now."

"Oh, Ned, that sounds like heaven. But will I feel like a deserter?"

"Of course you won't. I won't let you. Come, I know where I'm going to take you tonight." And we took a cab up to the Forty-ninth Street house.

By the end of the evening we had completed our plans: I would go back to school at once; we would spend as much time as possible getting the apartment ready, and as soon as it was habitable we'd be married.

"Why should we wait for the apartment, love? We could take a suite in a hotel and operate from there," Ned said, holding my face against his. "I could get a marriage license tomorrow—"

"No, Ned dear. That wouldn't be fair. We ought to wait a month or two—a month, at least. She was my mother, you know."

"Grace, if you knew how I need you—"

"And I you, darling. But let me tell the family; and then I won't feel so, well, as if I were being underhanded."

"On these conditions: that you set the soonest possible date, and that I see you every possible minute."

The familial responses to my news were more or less what I expected: Papa protested that I was showing no respect for the dead, Alfred and Ann were congratulatory, and Rose was noncommittal. Only Charles said he would miss me. Carrie, when I phoned her, was delighted. Once it was all out in the open, I felt easier in my mind, more honorable, one might say. I made an effort with Rose, persuading her to go shopping with me after school or to accompany Papa and the boys to the zoo. While she wasn't the chatty, ebullient person she had been just before Mamma's death, neither was she the recluse she'd been earlier. It was as if she had forgotten for a while whatever it was that tormented her, only to remember it again later in a different, controlled way. When I asked her how she passed all the time she spent in her room, her answer was evasive.

"I don't know. Sometimes I read. Sometimes I make a few notes. It's really my own affair, you know."

No wonder she objected to Miss Pomfret.

As for Papa, I couldn't do much for him. He had turned against me just as Mamma had after I moved out of Rose's room. Like her, I thought, he might get over it in time, but actually I didn't really care very much, especially after he made the outrageous suggestion that Ned and I live with him after we were married.

"You could have your old room, Grace, and Rose could move up a floor."

I think he knew that Alfred and his family would be leaving soon, and the prospect of a household reduced to himself and Rose was anything but pleasing. I don't know what Rose would have thought of such an arrangement, but it never came up. Ned, who was there the night Papa made his proposal, was too astonished to reply immediately, but when he did his refusal to consider any such suggestion was couched in terms so firm that my father said nothing further.

"How is Alfred's financial position now, Ned?" I asked after the others had retired.

"Not bad at all, as far as I can tell. The debts are just about cleared away. Of course, Ann's annuity helped there. He's in pretty good shape now; I find it hard to believe that he let himself get into such a jam—he always seemed too sensible to take risks in the market.

Anyway, it's over. I wouldn't be surprised if they set up on their own pretty soon."

"That's what Papa is afraid of, that he'll be left alone here with Rose."

"Look, love, you can do nothing about it. You're mine now, remember?"

Rose's light was out when I went up that night, so I didn't knock on her door, as I had been doing lately, to say goodnight. I didn't go directly to bed; my mind was full of plans for the apartment, so I spent some time at my desk making lists of things to be done. It was late when I finally went to sleep.

The next day, Rose's body was found in the moat of the Astor house. She had been stabbed in the throat.

18

After that, there was no way Papa could keep the police out of his home. Someone in the Astor house notified the authorities that a body lay in their areaway; a maid had spotted it from one of the kitchen windows. Of course, they didn't come to us immediately; no one knew who she was at first.

I'll put it all down as nearly as I can remember. The day was a cold, cloudy one in mid-February and started out like an ordinary Friday. Rose didn't appear for breakfast, but no one commented on her absence since she often slept late. Alfred left with the boys and me, and while I wasn't paying much attention to the conversation as the four of us walked to the corner together, I do recall their talking about the possibility of going ice-skating that afternoon. I was awfully tired; my head felt dull and achy from not having had enough sleep, and I was hoping they wouldn't ask me to go with them.

"If the white flag with the red ball on it is flying from the top of the Arsenal—and you can see it from here, you know—that means there's skating in the park," Alfred said as we reached Lexington Avenue.

It's not important at all, but I do remember that they did go skating; Lizzie took them. And it was just as well, because as soon as they were out of the house Papa told me that Rose was not to be found and that Maggie said her bed had not been slept in. I didn't know what to do; I thought Papa was in a state of shock, because he refused to answer any of my questions, but it was always hard to tell with him; it could have been that he was too angry to speak.

When Alfred came in and heard the news, he wanted to call the police immediately and report a missing person, but Papa would have none of it. He was infuriatingly adamant.

"There will be no publicity, no scandal, no noseybodies poking around my home. The indignity of it! And no one is to make a move unless I say so! Is that clear?"

I still can't believe it, but we took it from him. There we sat, Alfred and I (Ann had taken the children upstairs), two intelligent adults, accepting orders, however unreasonable, just as we had done when we were little. The "old obediences" that Mrs. Wharton speaks of in her memoirs must have been too deeply entrenched in our characters to permit defiance of parental authority. In the end, it was Carrie who reported Rose missing, and when the police phoned saying they had found someone answering Rose's description, she went with Alfred to identify the body.

The verdict at the coroner's inquest was murder by a person or persons unknown, and for several days detectives and policemen were in and out of the house. We were all questioned, separately and in groups, about Rose, her past life, her recent activities, her acquaintances, and so on.

Was some of my father's fear of public exposure handed down to us? It may well have been, because as far as I know, no one of us ever mentioned the internal difficulties of the family. The police never heard about the footsteps, real or imaginary, about our suspicions concerning Katie's death, Mamma's feeble last gesture, the hand on my shoulder, or the dead cat. Why we held all this back I was not sure. Now I attribute it to some hereditary reticence in us that prohibited disclosures that would be damaging to our public face. I also see now that we were behaving strictly in accordance with our Victorian upbringing, which is not to excuse our actions, but merely to try to explain them. I refer, of course, primarily to Alfred and myself, but I must not exclude Ann; she had been brought up to observe essentially the same rules, possibly even more stringent ones, since her family represented the old guard of Newport society.

Ned, too, was one of us, and although he was at the time nearly frantic about my safety, it never occurred to him to be other than circumspect in his replies to the few questions put to him. They were few, I suppose, in view of the fact that he was not a member of the family and had had little to do with Rose ever. He and I were both questioned closely in connection with the attempted break-in at the end of the summer before, but we could tell them no more in February than we had been able to in August. And of that they had a record.

The officer in charge of the case was Lieutenant Bondy, a soft-spoken, stolid, middle-aged man with hard, blue eyes and a shock of graying hair. He found it difficult to believe that we had no knowledge what-soever of Rose's life during the four years she had been away and that we could tell him next to nothing about Jack Egerton. He was also inclined to doubt our statements that my sister had never, at any time since her return, volunteered any information concerning that period. When, however, Dr. Bronson made his report on her condition (disassociation, nearing catatonia, a form of schizophrenia), the lieutenant appeared to be satisfied that we were telling the truth.

Of Egerton, he said, they could find no trace. He had no criminal record either in New York or any other city. And unfortunately no one could remember the name of his employer during the summer of 1916, if, in fact, it had ever been mentioned at all. The police had tried to locate his aunt, Mrs. Hollins, with no success. The brick house in East Quogue had been sold twice since it was built, and no one knew what had become of the original owners. Like Egerton, they had simply vanished.

"I think, Miss Millerton," he said one evening about two weeks after Rose's death, "that your intruder last summer was your sister's husband using her key. She may have told him the house would be closed up for July and August, as it had been in the past, so that part is easy. His motive? That could be one of many. Perhaps theft—she might have told him where to look for valuables. Or maybe he needed a place to hide, or even a night's shelter. The records show it was stormy that night, and if he was down and out that would fit. Are you sure there's nothing else you remember about him?"

I shook my head, and he remained silent for a moment before continuing.

"The only theory I have at present is that he had

some hold over her, so that she was forced to go out to meet him two weeks ago tonight. Who knows? She may still have been in love with him, a powerful motive for agreeing to meet him. Why he killed her is another unanswered question. We've ruled out robbery; she had a few dollars in her purse, which was found near the body, and a gold pin, worth quite a bit, I would say, was still on her dress. But we'll have no solution until we find Egerton."

"Or whoever else it was who killed her," Ned said.

"Yes, there's always that possibility," the lieutenant agreed as he prepared to leave. "We'll continue to keep a watch on the house, and I shall expect you to contact me immediately if you notice anything out of the ordinary."

His flinty blue eyes rested in turn on Alfred, Ann, Ned, and me; then he turned to Papa, who was staring into the fire.

"I shall not inflict my presence on you any longer, Mr. Millerton. Not unless or until there are further developments."

My father made no reply, and Alfred, obviously embarrassed by Papa's rudeness, got up to show the lieutenant out.

"And just you leave the cups for Lizzie McCabe, Miss Grace," Cook said as she poured hot, strong tea. "And there's more oatmeal cookies in the jar, should you be needing them. Goodnight to you now. I'll be going up."

After Papa had stamped angrily out of the parlor, Alfred suggested that we all go down to the kitchen.

"I feel as if I'd been in this room for days; come on, I'll make some tea."

But Cook was still there and insisted on waiting on

us. I regret that I can no longer take tea, even weak tea, at night; it's such a comforting drink, but nowadays it interferes with my sleep.

"Maybe Rose was behind it all," Alfred said suddenly. "She could have pushed Katie; remember how she stood at the top of the stairs? And it could have been her hand you felt, Grace, her footsteps you heard."

"But the cat, Alfred—"

"She could have done that, too. Maybe she had a grudge against Ann. She was half batty, anyway. Remember the glittery look in her eyes?"

"But she didn't stab herself, Alfred," Ned said, reaching out for my hand.

"No," Alfred answered slowly. "She couldn't have. But she could have been in touch with Egerton, and maybe Bondy's right about her still being in love with him, and maybe he was blackmailing her—"

"What would be the point?" I asked. "She had no money, or very little."

"He could have told her to get some, and then when she didn't have it—"

"What kept us from talking like this to the police?"

"It wouldn't do any good, Grace," Ann said. "It's all speculation, but in any case their interest is in finding Egerton, not in convicting Rose of killing Katie."

"Do you think Rose talked to herself? Miss Pomfret told Ned and me she heard voices in there one night."

"I think she might have done anything, unstable as she was. Come on, Ann, time for bed. Leave those cups, Grace. You heard Cook."

It was not without some qualms of conscience that I spent the greater part of the next day, Saturday, at the apartment, supervising the installation of draperies.

"Mrs. Kittredge is picking the boys up at eleven, Papa, and Alfred should be home for lunch," I said as I prepared to leave.

"Yes, yes, go on, go on, don't bother about me. Don't pay any attention to a decent period of mourning. Go on about your affairs. I don't know what the world is coming to." And once more he held the newspaper up so that I couldn't see his face.

I left, hoping Tom or Will or Carrie would drop in to see him. Carrie might, I thought, but about the other two I had my doubts. They were good-natured boys, and very willing, but not the most thoughtful. When I got home late in the afternoon, Maggie told me no one had called and that my father had spent the day going from one room to another, "as if he was looking for something, like."

"Didn't Alfred come home for lunch, Maggie?"

"That he did, Miss Grace, and then he was right off again. And Cook wants to know how many for dinner. Will Mr. Ned be coming?"

"No, I'm going out with him—oh, dear, that leaves only three for dinner, because Charles and Francis are with the Kittredges."

"She'll be that disappointed, Cook will. Shall I bring your tea now, Miss?"

"I'll take it up, Maggie. I'm going to my room to dress."

It wasn't like Papa to go wandering about the house; aside from a perfunctory inspection tour upon his return from the summer vacation, he rarely entered any rooms other than his bedroom, the front parlor, and the dining room, and those at stated times. Probably he just had nothing to do, I thought, and no one to talk to.

I would have thought twice about going out that

night, about risking my father's disapproval for the second time in one day, but Ned had been very persuasive, insistent, actually. Mrs. Cochrane would be returning from Miami shortly, which would put an end to our evenings in his study. And we'd not had many of them, none since Rose's death. Papa was barely civil to Ned when he called for me, but at least he refrained from commenting on what constitutes a "decent period of mourning."

Ned and I mourned for no one that night.

CHAPTER

19

The next day I found what my father must have been looking for. At lunch that Sunday he reiterated a request he had made once before: that I move back into my old room, and for the second time I refused. I suppose it did seem silly to have five people crowded together on the fourth floor, and only one in solitary splendor on the third, but the thought of occupying what had come to be known as "Rose's room" was, understandably enough, abhorrent to me. I didn't tell Papa that; I merely said that since I would be marrying Ned shortly and moving out altogether it hardly seemed worth the effort.

"In that case," he said, "would you be good enough to go through your sister's things, as you did your mother's, and clear everything away? I might use the room myself, have it fixed up as a study, or an upstairs sitting room. The light is good in there—makes it a more cheerful place than the parlor."

"I'll do it this afternoon," I said. "If Ned comes before I'm finished, ask him to come up." Papa's face registered disapproval at that, but he said nothing.

It didn't take me long to collect Rose's clothes and her few possessions. I packed them all up to give to the Little Sisters of the Poor, keeping only her gold pin, the one she was wearing when she was killed. I still have it, but, of course, I've never worn it. Perhaps I ought to give it to one of Carrie's girls, or maybe to Charles' daughter.

I was giving the empty closet a final check when I saw a remnant of the past that almost brought tears to my eyes. I'll have to explain: as the two youngest of the children, Rose and I depended almost entirely on each other for entertainment when we were little, and most of it we had to provide for ourselves. There was no television, not even radio, for passive enjoyment on long, rainy afternoons. Most of our games were made-up ones, not the board games Charles and Francis liked, and called for a fair degree of imagination.

I remember clearly how one day we were both sitting on the floor of the closet (marooned on a desert island and waiting to be rescued) when Rose poked at the wall next to her and dislodged a chunk of crumbling plaster. We picked away at the edges until we had an opening roughly three or four inches in diameter, and in time the hole became our cache and the nucleus of any number of games involving secret treasure, the crown jewels, coded messages, and such. We pasted a scrap of brocade from Mamma's rag bag across the top of the opening, and this served in turn as a tapestry, a tent flap, or whatever the game called for.

The brocade, faded to a nondescript gray, had been hidden by Rose's clothes, but it was still attached to the closet wall. I knelt down and lifted the little cur-

148

tain, wondering idly if I would come across any other vestiges of those days of innocence, but what I found belonged to the immediate past, days of deceit and tragedy. My fingers closed around a bulky white envelope, the kind used in business correspondence, instead of around the marble or hair ribbon I thought to find. I carried the envelope over to the window (there were no lights in any of our closets) and saw that it was addressed to me, just "Grace," in Rose's handwriting. Inside was a sheet of plain paper wrapped around a packet of money, all in new bills.

"I'll take that, Grace."

I hadn't heard my father come into the room, but when I turned away from the window he was standing quite close to me, with one hand outstretched.

"It's addressed to me," I began.

"But it does not belong to you," he said, taking the money from me. "I withdrew these funds from the bank for a personal reason that has nothing at all to do with you."

With that he stuffed the packet into an inner pocket and went down the hall to his own room, slamming the door behind him and locking it. At least it sounded as if he locked it. I was still standing at the window with the envelope in my hand when Maggie came up to tell me Ned was downstairs.

He was alone in the parlor when I went down.

"Where is everyone?" he asked, burying his face in my neck.

"Alfred took his family to the aquarium, and Papa's locked himself in his room."

"Come over here, then, love," he whispered. "I want you close, closer to me. That's it."

A little while later, when I heard Papa stirring in the room directly above us, I suggested that we go out. I had no desire to spend the rest of the afternoon in my father's company.

"Let's go for a walk, darling." I said. "And how about that tea at the Plaza you promised me?"

"One more kiss, and I'll buy you the best tea in the city!"

Once we were out of the house, I described to him the scene that had taken place in Rose's room.

"And there was no letter, no note?"

"Just the envelope with my name on it and the money. It looked like a substantial amount, wrapped in a sheet of plain paper—maybe she meant to write something on that."

"It looks to me as if your father had given the money to Rose, Grace. But why would she leave it behind when she left? If she was on her way to meet Egerton, and that's a likely supposition, wouldn't she have taken it with her? To start a new life, and all that?"

"None of it makes any sense, Ned. I can't help feeling that Ann is involved in some way; I know she's hiding something. Remember I told you how she went out alone one night, for a breath of air, she said, but I can't believe that. And then Rose gave me that message: 'Tell Ann it is not enough,' and when I delivered it, Ann said 'What nonsense' and ran upstairs. Maybe the money was really for Ann to give someone."

"It looks as if Egerton, or someone, was blackmailing both of them. I can almost understand his hold over Rose, Grace, but how Ann fits into it is beyond me. How would she have known him?"

"She met him that last summer in East Quogue along with the rest of us, Ned, but I can't remember that she ever had anything to do with him. He never came to the house for meals—we didn't know him well enough for that—and when he did come over he was always with Rose. Ann was there for only a month, and all her time was taken up with Charles and Francis because Alfred couldn't afford a nurse. That was when I began to think better of Ann; she never complained about anything."

"Well, then," he said, tucking my arm under his, "let's say that Ann may have something on her mind, but that it has no connection with Rose or Egerton, and let it go at that."

"Yes, Rose is gone, Papa has his money back, and Ann is flourishing, so maybe that's the end of it. Look at the skaters, Ned. Don't you think we ought to try it some day? I used to love ice-skating."

We stopped for a few moments at the edge of the Fifty-ninth Street lake to watch the Sunday skaters, some of whom glided serenely by, while others concentrated on staying upright as they took tentative steps out onto the ice. Rose and I had learned to skate on that lake, starting on double runners that the older children had discarded and working up to our own shoe-skates. I loved it, but she was never very good at it, and generally complained of the cold long before I was ready to go home.

I thought Ned had finished talking about the situation in the Sixty-fifth Street house, for we spent the next hour over an elegant tea discussing matters connected with the apartment. But I was wrong: he suddenly leaned toward me across the small table and put his hand over mine.

"Look at me, Grace. I've never been more serious in my life. I am not at all sure it is all over, and I'm more and more concerned about your safety. It occurs to me that Egerton was counting on that money; if so, he'll be back for it, and there's no telling to what lengths he'll go to get it. And you're so vulnerable, love. Alfred can take care of Ann, but you're alone. I'm convinced Egerton gets into the house one way or another, and if you should come upon him—good God, it's assumed he's killed once, and even if he hasn't, I feel you're not safe from him—"

"But what—"

"No, wait. Hear me out. Under no circumstances can I allow you to spend another night there, and this is what I propose: come stay with me tonight, and tomorrow morning we'll go down to City Hall and be married. I have the license—no, don't speak yet. If you're worried about the propriety involved, I'll get you a room at the Waldorf or here at the Plaza or any place you say, any place but your father's house. *Now*, what do you say?"

Suddenly I was frightened again; if Ned was right, and Egerton was counting on the money, then no one was safe in that house. All at once I could hear the footsteps again, feel the hand on my shoulder; I shuddered, and looked up to see Ned staring anxiously at me.

"Yes, darling, I'll go with you tonight. And I'm not in the least worried about the propriety involved," I said, and watched the look of relief that flooded his face.

"But I'll have to get some clothes, Ned—"

"Of course, love. We'll go and pick them up now, and I'll not let you out of my sight, not even while you're packing. If anything were to happen to you—"

20

I'll be safe now, I'll be safe, I kept saying to myself during the short taxi ride to Sixty-fifth Street, snuggled up against Ned's shoulder. No more footsteps, no more terror as I went down dimly lighted halls past closed doors, no more sleepless nights, no more Papa—oh, Papa—there was sure to be some kind of confrontation if he were to see me leaving the house with Ned carrying my suitcase. A final break, perhaps . . .

As the taxi approached the house, I automatically looked around for one of the policemen Lieutenant Bondy had detailed to keep an eye on us, but failed to spot either a uniformed patrolman or anyone who resembled a plainclothes detective. Over the past two weeks I had become accustomed to seeing one or the other.

"I don't see our watchman today, Ned."

"That's all to the good, darling. He wouldn't want to be conspicuous; he's probably behind one of the stoops having a smoke. I know Bondy hasn't called his men off yet, because I spoke to him yesterday."

I let us in with my key, and after hanging our coats on the old-fashioned mirrored clothesrack in the front hall, we went past the empty parlor and up the long flight of stairs. There wasn't a sound anywhere in the house; the maids, I assumed, were down in the kitchen preparing for dinner, and it looked as if Alfred and his family had not returned from the trip to the aquarium. The stillness, combined with the nature of our errand, was getting to me, and I held tightly to Ned's hand as we passed Rose's room. The door was wide open, but in the faint light of the gathering dusk little was visible of the room itself—just shadowy shapes of furniture, ominous, somehow in the semi-darkness. Papa's door was still shut; whether it was locked or not I had no idea.

We talked in low voices while I hurriedly packed the few things I could fit into the small suitcase I kept on my shelf. I didn't want to take the time to go down to the closet under the dining room stairs to look for a larger one. I just wanted to get out of that house as soon as I could. I had closed the suitcase, and Ned was in the act of picking it up when a noise from the floor above startled us both. It sounded like glass breaking, and a moment later we heard the pounding of feet on the stairs. Ned thrust me behind him, but I had a glimpse of a wiry figure, no more than a dark blur, as it shot past my door and down the hall. It had no sooner disappeared down the stairs than it was followed by a stockier figure in a blue uniform. It all happened incredibly fast; only a few seconds elapsed, I am sure, between the time they passed us and the time we heard the sound of the front door slamming.

A few minutes later, all of us—Maggie, Lizzie,

Cook, Papa, Ned, and I—were at the foot of the parlor stairs, where we found the front door wide open and no sign of either the pursuer or the pursued. I don't recall what Papa said to the maids, but they went back down to the kitchen. Then the three of us waited for some word from the police. After a while the panting officer returned, very red in the face, and asked to be allowed to use the telephone. Since we could hear only parts of the conversation, I will not attempt to reproduce it. After he hung up he gave us a report that went something like the following:

"He went in through the house next door, sir, up to the roof and across to your skylight. I'm afraid that's broken. Only reason I followed him in the first place was I didn't have him down as one of the regular occupants of the house. At first I thought he might be a visitor, but, then, he looked kind of seedy, you know. So I went after him, not letting him see me. But when he went on up to the roof I knew he was up to no good, and I nearly had him, but he went down through the skylight so fast, and I couldn't get through quick enough. But I would have caught him anyway if he hadn't slammed your front door in my face. That gave him time—I never saw which way he went, east or west. The lieutenant ain't gonna like this. He's on his way here now."

Needless to say, Ned and I couldn't leave then. When Bondy arrived, Ned told him he was reasonably sure the man was the same one he had run after the previous August, which served to confirm the lieutenant's theory that Rose had given Egerton her key sometime last summer and strengthened Bondy's belief that he had killed her.

"But what did he come back for?" Bondy asked.

Before Ned or I could tell him about the money, Papa spoke up.

"Who knows why a lunatic does anything? Probably he thought Rose had left some valuables here."

"If that were the case, why didn't he take her gold pin after he killed her?" asked Bondy.

Just then Alfred came in with his family, and after one look at the group of us in the parlor he sent his sons upstairs. Then the lieutenant went over the whole episode again for him and for Ann, who looked to be on the verge of collapsing.

"Will they never catch him?" she moaned. "Is there no end to this?"

"He'll be caught, ma'am," the lieutenant said grimly. "He's desperate now and likely to make a mistake. What I need is a description. Sullivan, did you get a good look at him?"

"Not too good, sir. I was behind him, you see. Like I said, he struck me as sort of seedy looking, shiny pants—"

"Hair color?" snapped Bondy.

"He wore a cap—couldn't see much, but it looked like it was gray or white. Like a cat, he was."

"Height?"

"Six feet or more, sir, and skinny."

"Coat?"

"No coat, sir. A heavy sweater of some sort, old looking. And tennis shoes, I think, and gloves."

"Weapon?"

"None that I could see, sir."

At that point Maggie came in to announce dinner, and when I looked questioningly at the lieutenant, he said to go ahead with our meal.

"If you don't mind, we'll go over the house again,

Miss Millerton, and after that there'll be two men watching the premises until further notice."

Papa protested, of course. Invasion of privacy, a man's house is his castle, by what right, all that sort of thing. But his bluster did him no good; Lieutenant Bondy stood his ground.

"Would you rather have your privacy invaded by the law or by the outlaw, sir?"

Papa gave him a withering look and strode out of the parlor, headed for the dining room stairs.

Dinner was awful. The little boys, naturally curious, were simply told that the police were looking for someone. They seemed more interested than alarmed. I suppose cops and robbers was only a game to them. Aside from them, Papa was the only one who gave any indication of relishing the food; the rest of us only picked at Cook's chicken à la king, and waited for the ordeal to be over.

I took hold of Ned's hand as we left the dining room, and as if he knew the question I wanted to ask, he bent over and whispered to me.

"Wait until the law leaves, darling, and then we'll go."

"He's left no clues," Bondy said as he prepared to go, "but you can rest assured that he won't get back in. I'll have two men here twenty-four hours a day, watching this house and the one next door. But you'd best put something over that skylight until you can get it fixed; a lot of cold air's coming in up there."

When he had gone, Papa stood at the parlor window grumbling to himself as he tried to spot the men left to guard us. Alfred and Ned were busy putting a temporary cover over the skylight, and Ann took the children up to bed. I went down to the kitchen to talk to the maids, to explain about the broken glass in their bathroom, and to assure them that the police were posted outside the house so no one could possibly get in.

"And what if he's still in the house, Miss Grace?" Maggie asked with a worried frown. I noticed she had the long-pronged toasting fork on the table near her hand, ready to take to bed, I thought.

"He escaped through the front door, Maggie, and then slammed it shut in the policeman's face to delay him. You can be sure he's outside, and that he won't get in again."

Lizzie looked anxious, Cook serious, and Maggie frightened. I couldn't blame any one of them. I wonder they didn't quit us then and there. But they didn't; they simply went on cleaning up and putting away the countless articles that have to be brought out for every meal, washed, dried, and restored to cabinet, drawer, or cupboard.

"Maggie, do you get those serving pieces back into the dining room; second drawer on the left of the sideboard, mind you." Cook was busy at the ice chest as she spoke, or she would have seen me smile when I saw Maggie take the toasting fork with her as she went toward the dining room. Had she been watching, Cook would have ordered her to hang that dangerous implement on the nail near the range, where it belonged.

"I'll go on up, then," I said, and started for the stairs. I never got there. As I passed the second of the built-in closets under the stairs, it occurred to me that I might as well take one of the larger suitcases up with me and pack a few more clothes. I pulled the wooden door open and found myself staring into the fierce, dark eyes of Jack Egerton.

In a second he had me twisted around in what I think is called the hostage position. He held me in front of him, the back of my head against his chest, and pressed something cold against my throat. For an eternity there was silence. Then he spoke.

"Scream, and it's the end. Feel this?" And the hoarse, harsh, whispering voice made what he said all the more terrifying.

"Walk," he commanded, propelling me slowly away from the kitchen and toward the areaway door. Later I realized that he intended to use me as a shield until he got safely past the policemen, but while it was happening I was too frightened to think of anything but the knife at my throat.

"Faster," he hissed as we neared the bottom of the stairs.

We passed the door to the dining room, and ahead of me I could see the boys' sleds standing up against the wall in the entry way. I was trying to think of a way of knocking one of them over with my foot, so that the noise of its falling would attract Maggie's or someone's attention, when Egerton suddenly gasped and let go of me so abruptly that I fell forward into the sleds. I caught myself just in time to turn and see him spinning frantically around with the toasting fork protruding from his back. He couldn't reach far enough to pull it out, and as Maggie and I backed away from him he fell on his face with a terrible crash and lay still.

21

"Egerton made a fool of young Sullivan," said Lieutenant Bondy, "simply by opening and then slamming the front door. After that he dashed down the dining room stairs. Since he did not have to pass the kitchen door to get to the closet he was not seen by the maids, all of whom were in the kitchen at the time. Nor would he necessarily have been seen had either of the maids been setting the dining room table when he swung around the bottom of the stairs to his left. The door leading from the hall to the dining room is just far enough forward of the stairs to enable him to keep out of sight of anyone in that room."

Egerton's body had been removed, Maggie had been put to bed with a sedative (which I refused), and the rest of us were gathered in Cook's big kitchen listening to the lieutenant's reconstruction of the chain of events.

"He must have known the house well, been familiar with every room, bathroom, all the doors and closets,"

Bondy continued, "and he probably acquired this knowledge by questioning his wife closely."

When he said that, I thought of all the times we had played long games of hide-and-seek, not only Rose and I, but also Tom and Will, and, on occasion, even Alfred and Carrie. What young child does not know all the hiding places in his own house? And those memories endure.

We were informed later that the experts agreed that the stab wound in Rose's throat was made by an instrument the size and shape of the one Egerton had held over me. And as far as the lieutenant was concerned, the case was solved, closed. Of course, there were things Bondy never heard about: the packet of money, the suspicions concerning Katie's death, the dead cat on Ann's dressing table—in fact, the whole Ann involvement, whatever it might be. And since he seemed satisfied with what he did know, we didn't volunteer any additional information.

Later, much later, after Bondy and his men had left, and after the rest of the household had retired, Ned took me home with him. We were married the next morning at City Hall, and went directly from there to a suite at the Plaza.

I kept in touch with Ann and Alfred by telephone, but I did not go back to the brownstone house until after we moved into the apartment, almost a month later. Ned went with me one Saturday morning, and while I was upstairs with Maggie helping me collect the books and things I wanted, he stayed down in the parlor with Papa, who was surprisingly cordial. My father was to take Charles and Francis to the Hippodrome that afternoon to see Houdini, and afterward to

Carrie's for dinner. He hadn't a worry in the world; he was king of his castle once more.

Most of my books had been left in Rose's room when I moved up to the fourth floor because of lack of space in the hall bedroom, and I was anxious to get them into my possession before Papa converted my old room into a study for himself.

"Will you be having room for all these in the new place, Miss Grace?" Maggie asked, pointing to the row of cartons we had lined up against the wall. I assured her I would, that we had a separate room just for books. She looked astonished and said she would like to see the "new place" some day.

After she went downstairs, I took a last look around, as I had the day I sorted Rose's clothes. I opened the door of the empty closet, and as on that previous occasion, knelt down and felt around in the cache. The pieces of paper I found in the bottom of it must have been underneath the envelope that contained the money; there were several sheets folded together, lined paper, torn out of a composition book. They were, I knew, the "notes" Rose once told me she was making. I slipped them into my purse and didn't mention them until Ned and I were back in our apartment. I've copied them out, so that this record will be complete.

22

By the time you read this, Grace, and I'm sure you'll be the one to find it, because you're the only one who ever knew about our old secret cache, I will have left again, this time for good. I never did want to come back to this house, but I had no choice. Remember how someone in Zola's *Germinal* said that a girl will always go back to the man who first had her? (What would Mlle. Pardeau have said if she had known that a group of her young ladies were reading that instead of "Le Jongleur de Notre Dame"? Or that Thérèse Tissault had sneaked the book out of her father's library? I still giggle when I think of it.) Anyway, that is the case with me. I am going back to Jack as soon as the moment is right.

But I have things to tell you first.

I had better begin at the beginning. We moved around a lot during the four years I was away, from one city to another, always big cities, because Jack said it's easier to be anonymous there than in a small town. Things went pretty well for a while, and we had enough money. We were in Chicago at first; he did some kind of work—I'm not sure what it was—but then that winter was awfully cold, and his bronchitis came back. He got sick and lost the job. So we went south and from then on moved around so much that I scarcely remember where we were at what time. It was always the same. He'd get work, keep it for a while, and then either get bored or dissatisfied or be let go (although he seldom admitted that).

Oh, I forgot: we changed our names in each city. That was his idea, not mine. Somehow or other we always had enough food and a roof over our heads, and maybe things would have worked out in the end except that I got sick. You've seen me sick. I don't know what it is, but this awful depressed feeling comes over me, and lasts and lasts, and then it goes away. I think I'm better now, but I don't know for sure.

The only thing that worries me is that Jack is so different. But even so . . .

As far as I know, he never broke the law or did anything dishonest while I was with him, but I'm not so sure of that now. It started last summer when we were living in Jersey City. He had a job in a factory, but the conditions were awful, the heat and all, so he left. And by that time we had almost no money. We lived in a horrid rooming house, the worst I've seen, and one afternoon when I was lying on the bed (I didn't feel well) Jack picked up my purse from the dresser and dumped everything out of it. That was when he found the key to this house. For some reason I had always hung on to it, the one to the front door, not the areaway. I never used the lower door, I hated going in or out that way, so I threw that one away long ago. He knew I wasn't asleep, but I don't think he knew I saw him put the key in his pocket. Then he counted the coins in the change purse, seventy-six cents, and said he was taking two quarters. He told me he had to go out, but wouldn't say where. He came back very late that night, soaking wet, and the next day he was sick again with bronchitis.

I overheard you talking to the others about an intruder. (I overheard much more than that.) Of course, it was Jack. He never told me, but it must have been. I guess he was going to steal something—I don't know. In a few days he went back to the factory. He looked awful, so white and thin. I didn't want him to go to work, but he said he had to even if he felt tottery. We needed the money. You see, for a while he used to get money in the mail, but then it stopped coming. Then sometime in November, when it began to get cold, I was miserable. I began, as usual, when one of those low periods is coming on, not to care about anything, and when Jack told me I had to come back here I just did what he said.

He promised to come and get me when he was on his feet again, and then he brought me here. He waited across the street in the Taylors' areaway until Maggie opened the door. I didn't want him to leave me here. I never liked this house, and now I hate it. And I wanted to be with him.

I didn't hear from him for a long time, not until just before Christmas, when someone forgot to close the areaway door all the way. Of course, you had had the locks changed, so my old key was of no use, and he had to watch for a chance to get in some other way. He stayed just inside the door until the coast was clear and then he came upstairs. He knew where our old room was—he had often asked me questions about the house—and came right to me. I hid him in the bathroom for a while, and then told him to go up and hide in the storeroom. He had some tools, and later he fussed with the lock so that Mamma's key wouldn't work.

Oh, I can't write it all—

(There is a break in the writing here.)

Now I'll go on. I didn't know what to do; what could I do? I didn't feel well, either. I don't feel too well right now, but I'm not really sick.

Anyway, Jack managed to stay hidden. The maids were never up on the fifth floor during the day, so he was safe then. But he didn't stay there all day every day; he'd go out because he was afraid if he were up there all the time the chances of his being discovered were greater. He said he sometimes went into museums to keep warm, or to churches. He'd come down at night—I'm so glad you moved out of this room— and I'd give him the food I'd saved for him. Sometimes he'd sleep here, in my bed, and make love to me. It was hard when the Pomfret was around.

You know the skylight in the maids' bathroom? He worked out a way of going and coming through that. He could cross the roof to the house next door, where there's a real door onto the roof, and go down their stairs. It isn't as if a family lives there; it's just flats and rented-out rooms, so the doors were apt to be closed, and he was careful about what times he came and went. I guess he was lucky, too, because he never met anyone there except a woman cleaning the hall, and she must have thought he lived there, because all she said was good morning. Most of the tenants there work and are away all day, so that helped.

That's how he brought the cat in. He said it was

dead when he found it, and he put the picture wire (that was in the storeroom) around its neck to scare Ann into paying him to be quiet about something he knew. I guess it was Ann who sent the money in the mail for a while. I knew what it was, too. Remember East Quogue? And how Ann used to go off with Charles and Francis every day? To the beach or to pick berries? Well, what she really did was to leave the children with a woman in the village and then she'd meet Jack someplace. They had an affair; I suspected it at the time, and he told me later it was so, but I loved him so much I let it go. Anyway, it was all a long time ago, and I still love him. He went to the bookstore to get her to give him money, or he met her at lunchtime. I never liked Ann, so I didn't care if he did scare her. Besides, what could I do?

But, Grace, he did *not* push Katie down the stairs. She saw him come out of the hall door to the bathroom when she was taking the tray down, and he must have frightened her so that she missed her step. He had gone into the bathroom to eat what I had saved for him; I don't know why he came out that door, perhaps he thought Katie was gone. She must have thought he was a ghost, he was so pale, and his hair is going white, too. He said it was just as well that Katie was out of the way because he thought she might have seen him the day you went up to the storeroom.

You remember that day; you made me angry by asking who I'd been talking to the night before when the Pomfret woman was snooping. Jack was hiding in the bathroom again; his throat was bad, and he didn't want to go out that day because the weather was so raw. I was sad, though, that Mamma had to die . . .

I'm nearly through. It's all over, and I'm going. I have the money now. It happened like this, and knowing Papa and his ways as you do, you won't be too surprised. You know how seldom he spent any time with me, don't you? He hardly ever came to my room, so I never expected him, but that day—about a week ago—he barged in and Jack didn't have time to hide in the closet or under the bed or in the bathroom.

You can imagine the brouhaha. It was incredible. But finally Papa said he would pay us, *us*, not just Jack, five thousand dollars to clear out once and for all, and made us sign a paper. He told Jack to leave at once or he'd call the police (I knew he'd never do that, though) and said he'd get the money and give it to me, and that I would have to go, too. I didn't want to take the money, but Jack said we had to have it. Papa gave it to me yesterday.

(Once again there is a break in the writing.)

I can't face it. I do love him, but how can I go back to that kind of life? And I feel another low period coming on, too. I can't go through with it. I'll tell him tonight, when I meet him where he told me to be. And if I give the money back to Papa maybe he'll let me stay. Staying here—yes, I'd be better off that way. At least I'll be warm and dry. I feel awful. Maybe I'll feel better later on. Oh, Grace, I don't know what to do.

23

N ed and I were both silent for a few minutes when we finished reading what Rose had left for me to find. I felt completely drained and at the same time wretchedly guilty for not having done more for her when she was so miserable and so mixed up. I could have tried harder to help her, even though I'd come to resent her presence; I just didn't make the effort.

"So, when she showed up without the money Egerton killed her, out of rage, probably," Ned said after a while. "We'll have to accept that, love. If she had given him the money things might have been different, but, poor girl, she thought she had to return it to your father because she wanted to stay. She was torn—"

We agreed that no useful purpose would be served by showing Rose's notes to anyone. Ann never knew that we knew that Egerton had been blackmailing her. When I reminded Ned of the conflicting stories my brother and his wife had told about the thousand-dollar-a-month annuity, he said Ann was forced to lie, not only because she'd been paying Egerton to keep him quiet, but also because of her fear of the consequences of exposure.

"It was when she turned the money over to me to help settle the debts that things got tough," Ned continued. "But even before that she had, according to Rose, stopped sending anything to Egerton. Maybe Ann thought it had gone on long enough, that the affair was well in the past—I don't know. In any case, she had some reason to cut off the payments sometime last summer. But she hadn't counted on Egerton's desperate need, or his persistence.

"There was a lot at stake for Ann, Grace, her marriage for one thing. She does love Alfred, anyone can see that, and the affair with Egerton meant nothing really. She probably fell into it out of boredom. And also, think how the elder Kittredges would have reacted had Alfred divorced her. They're even more straitlaced and reactionary than the Victorians. They'd be disgraced socially (in their own eyes, at least) and Ann would be disinherited, probably ostracized.

"She lied to you confidently, darling, knowing you were too well bred and delicate to embarrass her by asking too many questions. The stupid thing she did was to run up so many bills; that was a frantic gesture of bravado, or it could be that she simply didn't care at that point. Anyway, she's done a complete turnabout, and the marriage is working. It would be most unfair of us, and completely unnecessary, to ever let those papers of Rose's come to light."

"I hope Papa got rid of whatever paper he made Rose and Egerton sign," I said. "Maybe he did when he got the money back. It was strange, wasn't it, that he had a suspicion that Rose hadn't taken the money with her? I suppose it was because he saw that she was reluctant to take it in the first place."

"Even if it did show up it couldn't hurt anyone now. Come over here, Mrs. Cochrane, and admire our own private view of the park at dusk. And then let's have a drink, and write *finis* to the whole sad business."

CHAPTER

24

Alfred and Ann moved that summer to a spacious apartment on Madison Avenue. I think my brother felt somewhat guilty about leaving Papa alone, since he'd been kind enough to take them in when they needed it, but Ann's happiness came first. As it turned out, my father was not alone for any length of time; he died in his sleep that September a few days after returning from a summer in the mountains. The brownstone house, along with whatever furnishings the heirs did not want, was sold soon after his death, and as I said earlier, the new owner made it over into flats.

Cook went back to Ireland to live with some relatives, and Lizzie McCabe married a policeman whom she met through young Sullivan. Maggie was not tried for the murder of Jack Egerton; the grand jury returned a verdict of justifiable homicide. When I invited her to come to work for us, she said she would, provided we had no toasting forks in the "new place."

Soon after we were married, Ned's mother moved to

Florida permanently. Now that Ned was settled, she said, she felt free to pamper her arthritis in the warm southern sun. Perhaps that's what she had had in mind the day she annoyed me so by playing matchmaker. We went to see her occasionally over the years, but neither of us liked the glare of Miami. She seemed glad to see us whenever we did go and never complained about the infrequency or the brevity of our visits; she was either a very good woman or a very selfish one—I could never decide.

We had our delayed honeymoon in Switzerland, the first of many luxurious trips abroad, and in the fall of 1922 I gave up teaching for a while in order to concentrate on completing the requirements for the master's degree. Ned, like Carrie, encouraged me to go on for the doctorate, which I received in 1930, and which led to a tenured professorship at Hunter College. I was immeasurably glad that I had that after Ned died of a heart attack in 1952. These past nine years without him have been lonely ones and would have been absolutely unbearable had I not had my work.

It was after his death that the recurrent dreams began. At first the headaches that followed were fairly mild, but as time went on they became progressively more intense. I don't see how Ned's presence could have prevented them, but it must have. I always felt so secure, so safe, when he was with me. Perhaps, though, Dr. Bronson prescribed the right treatment for me: I've noticed that since I started on this record the dreams and headaches have been more infrequent; maybe if I include *everything* I remember about Rose's death they'll stop completely.

The night she left the house, the night she died, I was up late making lists in connection with the readying of the apartment. Ordinarily I would not have heard the noise that precipitated my action, but it was after midnight when I put down my pen, and the house was deathly still. I had opened the drawer of my desk to put my lists away when my glance fell on the wretched letter opener I had foolishly allowed Charles to buy, and it was while I was wondering how to dispose of it safely that I heard the unmistakable sound of the front door closing.

Just as I had known that it would be Rose who was in the parlor on Thanksgiving, so I knew it was she who went out that night. I snatched the letter opener from the drawer—I can't imagine why I thought I would need a weapon to bring her back—and my purse from the dresser and flew down to the floor below. Rose's door, which had been closed tight when I passed it earlier, was open about six inches. I didn't stop to investigate; I knew she wasn't in there. I certainly wasn't thinking clearly; I should have called Alfred to help me, but my one idea was to go after her and bring her back, and besides, it would have taken too long to get him out of bed.

I paused at the top of the stoop to see which way she had gone, and at first I didn't see any sign of her. Then, when my eyes became adjusted to the darkness of the street I made out a slim figure moving slowly in the direction of Park Avenue. I almost caught up with her at the corner of Madison and would have done so if I hadn't had to wait for a trolley car to pass. She crossed to the north side of Sixty-fifth Street and went toward Fifth Avenue, still walking slowly, almost strolling along as if she had no purpose or destination in mind. Halfway down the block a man appeared from behind one of the stoop posts, and they walked together in the direction of the park. They paused next to the railing at the Astor house, near the gate to the tradesmen's entrance. A moment later, the man, Egerton, of course, began to beat her about the head.

Neither one of them saw me at first, and as I rushed toward them I heard Rose gasp something that sounded like "No, no, it's not here." She meant the five thousand dollars, of course, but I didn't know that then. My only thought at that moment was to make Egerton stop hurting her. In the struggle that followed, I tried to pull him away from her, but he was a man possessed, and I doubt that he knew I was there until I began to slash at him with the letter opener. I must have hurt him, because he let go of Rose with one hand and turned on me. I was trying to cut his other hand (the one holding Rose) with my weapon, but his right arm came up so suddenly and so powerfully that my own arm was deflected and the deadly little instrument sank deeply into Rose's throat.

She fell against the gate in the railing, and when the weight of her body caused it to swing open she tumbled down the stone steps and lay still in the moat. As I looked down at her Egerton wrenched the letter opener from my hand. I thought he was going to attack me with it and tried to cry out. I couldn't; I couldn't make a sound. Then he turned away from me and ran toward the darkness of the park.

I went home. I have no recollection of how I got there.

The next few days were bad. I couldn't risk telling anyone I had followed Rose that night; my whole future was at stake. I don't think I would have gone to prison, but there would have been a trial, or at least an investigation. I might not have lost Ned, but his feeling for me might have changed, and I couldn't bear the thought of not having him cherish me the way he did.

And of course the Millerton image would have been smudged.

Jack Egerton was responsible for three deaths, but he did not kill anyone. I did.

Yesterday Dr. Bronson asked me to marry him. When I refused, he did not seem too upset. He merely rubbed his forehead and sighed.

"Perhaps you're right, Grace," he said. "But I should like to see you, go out to dinner, the theater, that kind of thing. Everyone needs a companion. Keeps the loneliness at bay."

Well, we'll see.